ABBEY OF THE DAMNED
THE COMPLETE CASES OF MIKE
& TRIXIE, VOLUME 3

ABBEY OF THE DAMNED

THE COMPLETE CASES OF MIKE & TRIXIE, VOLUME 3

T.T. FLYNN

ILLUSTRATRATIONS BY

JOSEPH A. FARREN

POPULAR PUBLICATIONS · 2025

TABLE OF CONTENTS

BARRED DOORS

Mike Harris Was Looking for a Half Million in Missing Bonds, but the Trail Led to the Body of a Strangled Woman in a House of Mystery

1

THE MISSING TRUST FUND

"KELLY," I CALLED to the big Swede behind the bar, "make the next one a *kummel.*"

Don't ask me how a Kelly came out of Sweden. This one did. Every time he opened his mouth you knew it. Kelly looked over at my table. His eyes were bulging.

"Kummel," he says. *"Kummel,* Mr. Harris?"

"You heard me. *Kummel.*"

"But," Kelly croaked, "de last one vas an absinthe drip. An' before dat she vas dis Mexican *tequila.*"

"I want *kummel.*"

"Mr. Harris," says Kelly with a moan, "absinthe and *tequila* she is planty for any faller. But not *kummel* too, Mr. Harris. Vas you Samson herself *kummel* with all the rest would kill you."

"Kummel," I says to Kelly. "If I have to come over there and pour it myself."

"Yumpin' yiminy," says Kelly, and brings me *kummel.*

So I drank *kummel* while Kelly stood there with his big mouth hanging open. "Mr. Harris," he says, shaking his head. "Neffer have I seen it. No, neffer."

"Which goes to show," I told Kelly, "that life will always have something new for you. I'm celebrating, Kelly."

"What?" says Kelly with a deep breath.

"My vacation. I've gone traveling. No more work. I'm free as a butterfly. Le's see, what country will we visit next? Russia, hey Kelly? How about some *vodka?*"

"Ooch!" Kelly winced.

"Make it a big *vodka,*" says I expansively. "It's an international celebration, Kelly. Around the world on thirty bottles—or watch Mike Harris get a vacation one way or another. *Vodka,* you big Swede, before I climb on a chair and look you in the eye."

"If I die for it, Mr. Harris," says Kelly tearfully, "not *vodka.* No, not if I bane lose my yob."

Before I could argue about Kelly's job, Thompson walked

*"Hold it!" I said, as Trixie
moved in behind me*

in, took one look and planted himself at my table. He was red-faced and sore.

"Mike, have you been drinking?" Thompson demanded coldly.

I put Thompson in his place with dignity. "I'm on my vacation," I told him. "Traveling. Jus' about to enter Russia. Passports in order an' the Red Guard ready to s'lute. Join me in a *vodka*."

Kelly covered his eyes and went away from there; and Thompson jerked out a cigar, bit off the end and jammed the cigar in the corner of his mouth.

"I've been looking all over for you. Three hours I've been looking, with half the men in the local office doing the same."

"Hurray for the local office," says I. "If they can't find one

Shoulder high his hands went

of their own men, what a swell bunch of dicks they must be. Call 'em in an' we'll all have *vodka*."

Thompson's face grew red.

"I'm not a drinking man!" he snapped. "This is the first time in years I've seen you take a drink, Mike!"

"It's the first time in years I've had a vacation. Kelly, two *vodkas*. Quick, you catfish-jawed Swede!"

"This is a sorry sight," Thompson delivered himself angrily. "I've got a notion to fire you, Mike!"

"I quit," says I. "Fire somebody else. Kelly, you're straining my disposition!"

THOMPSON ROLLED HIS cigar across his mouth and chewed hard on it. "Hell! You haven't quit and you aren't fired, Mike. I've got a job for you."

"Not me!"

"I need you," says Thompson. "I was counting on you, Mike. You've never let me down yet. Not going to start it now, are you?"

"I don't hear you. Kelly...."

"Mike!" says Thompson, catching my sleeve. "This is a big job. Important as hell. D'you think I'd pound sidewalks and pay taxi fares for three hours trying to find you if it was a gag? Brace up; listen to me."

He had me. He knew he had me. Thompson forgot to chew his cigar as he watched me slipping. "I was all set to throw one big bust, come hell or high water," I groaned. "Can't you let me find a good gutter in peace?"

"I need you, Mike."

"I'm drunk."

"Go to a Turkish bath and sweat it out, and then come to

the office as quick as you can. Here, I'll take you to the bath myself."

Kelly beamed behind the bar as Thompson guided me out.

Maybe you don't know me; Mike Harris of the Blaine Agency, redheaded and not too big but I always let the other fellow worry.

Mike Harris

The Blaine International Agency, in case you've never heard about it either, rates. Plenty. Our offices are spotted from 'Frisco to Shanghai, New York to Bombay and points between. Anything taken, one man or a thousand on the job, if your rating justifies the bill; and everything goes to get results.

Results! Thompson lived for that. He was manager of the eastern division, headquarters in New York. Mostly I worked out of his office; but over a year's time I barnstormed everywhere. They worked me to death, gave me no rest, promised me vacations and scrambled the vacations when I started them.

Like now.

I boiled out in the Turkish bath and taxied to Thompson's office. He was waiting for me, the same cigar or its brother cocked in one side of his mouth. A man stood beside the desk.

"How do you feel?" Thompson demanded.

"So-so."

"Meet Sir Douglas Carter MacClain. This is Michael Harris, the best man we have for this business, Sir Douglas."

Sir Douglas gave me a ramrod bow from the hips. He was stiff, starchy, crochety in appearance, with the look of a man who would be hell and high water to soldier under. His face was beet-red from sun and exposure, his mustache was stiff and bleached to a straw color. Frosty blue eyes scanned me with a shade of disapproval. He nodded without saying anything, sat down stiffly and left Thompson to do the talking.

Thompson did, succinctly. "Sir Douglas has just lost half a million dollars, Mike."

"A hundred thousand pounds," Sir Douglas corrected coldly. He fiddled with the end of his mustache, eyed us both severely. Plain to see he didn't have much use for detectives or the business that brought him here.

So I said: "A hundred thousand pounds? Fancy! Where was it mislaid?"

Sir Douglas snorted.

Thompson scowled past his cigar. Once he took a case he was in it up to his eyes. Sometimes I believe he suffered as much as his clients.

"The money was stolen," Thompson said curtly.

"Can't the police get any trace of it?"

SIR DOUGLAS SNORTED again and glared at me. "Dammit, my good fellow, that is why I am here! I can't, hrmmmph, afford to have the law look into this matter. My career, my reputation, demn it, the honor of my family, are involved. If you're to handle this, I want it understood there is to be no publicity. You understand, no publicity?" He eyed me as if he thought I might have designs on the family honor.

Trixie Meehan

Thompson put in hastily:

"It's this way, Mike; Sir Douglas has had charge of a trust fund of a couple of million dollars. Had it under his wing for some years. All in gilt edge securities which needed little watching. His secretary did most of the paper work.

"But it seems," said Thompson—and was I mistaken in thinking he was picking his words carefully—"that a business associate of Sir Douglas, conniving through the secretary, got his hands on a half million dollars' worth of the trust funds and departed."

"A hundred thousand pounds!" Sir Douglas snapped.

"A hundred thousand pounds," Thompson agreed smoothly. "We're going to get it back, Mike."

"Maybe," I gave Thompson, shrugging.

Sir Douglas Carter MacClain glared at me.

"Am I to understand you already expect to fail?" he asked me loudly. "Thompson, you assured me this man was practically infallible, and here, dash it, he speaks of failure before he starts!"

"A poor choice of words, Sir Douglas," Thompson said quickly, giving me the cold eye.

So to MacClain I said: "I'll get your money if it's getable. Where was it stolen from?"

"Here; here in New York," says Sir Douglas. He rolled it out nastily from under his brushy mustache, as if the Big Town gave him an acute pain.

"Where?"

"From my office; from the safe in my office!"

"You had a half million in your office safe?"

"Demn it, yes! Perfectly all right there. Never been bothered before. The office door hasn't even a name to suggest valuables might be within."

"What is your business?" I asked him.

Sir Douglas screwed a monocle in his eye and dressed me down with a look.

"I am an investor," he said. "And ahh, hrmphh—speculator. Quietly, of course; unknown to the public. I repeat, the contents of my safe were not attractive to any one."

So I slipped him a dry barb on that. "Obviously," says I cheerfully. "You lost only half a million. Cash, or how?"

"In your—er—American Liberty Bonds."

Did I whistle low then? I did. "Liberties? Were they registered?"

His face grew redder. "They were not!" he replied stiffly.

I looked up at him, looked at Thompson, fished out a cigarette, and rolled it between my palms slowly. I'd seen all kinds of people; I'd heard all sorts of stories, and I'd come to the point where I could detect a rotten odor so faint the ordinary person would never get it. So I fished.

"It still seems to me," says I blandly, "that the police

should have a look at this. They're good in their way; they can trace Liberties where, possibly we couldn't."

I thought Sir Douglas was going to have pups. He swelled up and his face ripened under a rush of blood as he exploded:

"I made myself clear about that! I will not have the police until I have exhausted every other resource! I want no publicity, no newspaper headlines! Lately I have sustained losses of my own money! I might be accused of having knowledge of this! It—damme man!—might even be said that I had borrowed from this trust fund! Another suggestion like that, sir, and I will take my business elsewhere! I am willing to pay handsomely for expert assistance, but I will not be badgered about the police! Positively, I will not! D'you understand? I will not!"

I GATHERED HE did not want the cops.

Thompson leaped in to save a fat fee.

"Sir Douglas is quite right, Harris. Not another word about the police. What are we in business for?"

I bowed (so help me, I bowed) and smoothed it pronto. "My error," I back-pedaled. "No cops in on this, hey? Not a cop. We won't need 'em. What makes you think your secretary got the bonds?"

Sir Douglas cleared his throat. His eyes had a fishy look. I had a growing idea that if his trust fund accounts were taken apart the smell would get worse. But, so far, that was his business. He disposed of the secretary promptly enough.

"I have been in Montreal several days; went for a week and returned unexpectedly this morning. Price, my secretary, wasn't in the office. I thought nothing of it at first, until I discovered that the safe had been looted. In some way Price had obtained the combination."

"He didn't know the combination before?"

"Emphatically not, sir! He obtained it in some under-handed manner. And now the young bla'guard is gone!"

"Hmmm," says I. "Wasn't that a dirty trick! You seem certain he did it, Sir Douglas."

"Why not?" he snapped at me. "I have proof. I went at once to Price's rooming house. He had left; decamped bag and baggage day before yesterday afternoon, leaving no forwarding address. A man had gone with him. The landlady described the man so clearly that I recognized a certain Colonel Humphries with whom I have been conducting some business negotiations."

Sir Douglas snorted. "There's no doubt that my safe was looted by those two rascals! I want them apprehended. Umphh—I mean to say, I want the bonds recovered."

"If that's all," I suggested, "maybe it won't be so hard. Often stuff is lifted that way for the reward. A little cash for bait might get a quick nibble."

He brushed the idea aside.

"Impossible! I have not the money. Any sum deducted from the estate funds would have to be explained, thereby making the whole matter public."

I thought: "Play the hog and you'll drown in your own mud puddle." But I said, "All right, describe your secretary and this Colonel Humphries. Everything you can think about them."

He did. It wasn't much; and he had the nerve to wind up with, "When can I expect results in this matter?"

I passed the buck with a solemn face. "Mr. Thompson will handle the end of it. He gives the orders and the publicity."

So Thompson eased him out through the front office, salving him all the way, and I sat on a corner of Thompson's desk and wondered what the straight of this business was. Half a million was nobody's sneer. A dumb secretary wouldn't snatch that and run if he had a nitwit's brain. He couldn't keep his tracks covered a week after the hue and cry was raised.

Thompson reentered the room and I yammered, "Five hundred grand tossed down the spout and he doesn't tell enough about it to get back a lost poodle! Do you really expect me to dive in and come up with his bundle of Liberties? My great-aunt Hetty! Liberties—and not even registered!"

Thompson rubbed his palms together and applied a match to his cigar.

"Certainly, Mike, my boy," he assured me calmly. "That's what we're here for."

"*We?* What have you got to suggest about it?"

"It's all yours, Mike. I have the greatest confidence in you. If you fall down on it, I'll step in and do something."

The hell of it was Thompson would probably do just that. He wasn't boasting. He'd cracked enough cases in his day to last a lifetime.

"Gimme an order for a hundred bucks expense money," I growled.

Thompson wrote the order without batting an eye—which showed where he stood on this. Usually Thompson crabbed and moaned over every extra dime. When he didn't you could be pretty sure the case was important and the sky the limit.

I took the order upstairs to the cashier, got four twenties, a ten and two fives, and went out to grab Price's trail at his rooming house.

2

A WOMAN SCORNED

SIR DOUGLAS MACCLAIN had given me the rooming house address. It fitted the type of fellow who would meekly—he'd have to be meek—take orders from a blustering windbag like MacClain.

Price had lived in the lower twenties. It was an old red brick rooming house, three stories high, set in a row of similar houses like a cracker in a box. The front steps were worn down from generations of roomers who had trudged in at night and trudged out in the morning; When I rang the doorbell it sounded harsh and off-key inside.

Steps came from the back, solid, determined, unhurried. Before she opened the door I knew what the landlady would be like. She was. An Amazon, no less. A head taller than me, with big, fat shoulders, she bulged out in wider hips, and down in tent-like canopy of black skirts to shapeless black shoes cracked over the toes. Her sagging face was sour and colorless. A curling iron had worked so long and hard on her coarse black hair that it looked like a black wig, dusty and lifeless. Maybe it was a wig at that.

She eyed me warily, half coyly, half forbiddingly.

"If you've come to look at that room I advertised today, you got here quick," she said.

"Sorry," I said. "I have a room. No doubt you'll rent yours by dinner time. I came here to ask you—"

She started to slam the door. I got my foot in just in time and followed it up with a shoulder.

"Wait a minute, lady! I'm not trying to sell you anything. I'm here on business. Get me? Business!"

"I haven't any money to spend if that's on your mind!" She stood there in the half-gloom of the hall, snapping through six inches of open doorway; and I talked fast before she left me outside talking to a blank door.

"I'm looking for some information about a chap named Price who roomed here. Don't tell me he didn't, because he did; and don't tell me you don't know anything, because it won't get by!"

"Say, who're you talking to?" she snapped back. "The nerve of a little shrimp standing on my own door step an' telling me off! Get your foot out of that doorway, young man, before I throw you out with my own hands! I've handled better men than you!"

"I don't doubt it, lady," said I. "You look like you've been through plenty. But this ain't your day for tossing anybody. And if you run off that mouth of yours much more I'll take you around to the precinct station, and let you have a real chance to talk."

She batted her eyes. "You a policeman?" she asked, deflating.

"What do I look like?" says I, letting her think whatever she chose.

"Why didn't you say so?" she said plaintively, opening the door again. "How's a woman to know one of you plainclothesmen, unless you speak up? I'm bothered all day by peddlers an' bums. A poor woman who's trying to live by taking in a few roomers can't afford to take chances. What was it you wanted to know about Price? I can't tell you much."

"He lived here, didn't he?"

"He had a room five or six months. I never would have thought such a quiet, refined young man would get into trouble this way."

"Who said he was in trouble?"

"What would everybody be askin' questions so for if he wasn't in trouble? First his boss comes this morning. I could tell there was something wrong by the way he talked. An' now it's the police wantin' to find out about him."

THE ONLY WAY to handle this old bulldog was to give her better than she handed out, so I said: "Never mind any trouble Price is in. He went off with another man, didn't he?"

"Yes, sir. I told his boss that. Went off in a taxi, they did. The other man walked up an' down on the sidewalk while Price ran up to his room and packed. 'I'm leaving for a week or so, Mrs. Simpson,' says he. 'Here's the next two weeks' rent in advance, and you can hold my mail.'"

"Where did he say he was going?"

"He didn't," she told me. "I asked him an' he made out like he didn't hear. And me not being a prying woman, I didn't ask more. He left some clothes in his room, but they ain't much. If he hadn't paid in advance I'd have his room rented by now."

"Let me have a look at his room."

She didn't think about demanding a search warrant. We

went upstairs, and she stood in the doorway while I made a quick search.

Price's room was small, badly lighted, stuffy. He had left a few old shirts and some underclothing in the drawers of an old marble-topped dresser. In a clothes closet I found an old gray suit and a pair of worn-out shoes. That was all. Nothing to indicate where he had gone or why.

"What about Price's friends? Who came to see him?"

"No one ever came here to see him. He was quiet and retiring like."

"Any mail come for him?"

"Not a letter," she said. "But I wrote down the telephone number of his girl. The way he did her dirt I'm surprised he paid me in advance. He must have been a bad one, mister. If he comes back and you want me to call the precinct station, I'll do it."

"Never mind that right now. Where's this telephone number you wrote down? And how do you know it was his girl?"

"I've been a mother. I've got a woman's intuition. You could tell by her voice she was a sweet young thing he'd taken advantage of. Even if she did swear a little it was no more'n a girl in her place would do. He ran out on her cold, it seems. If I was this Lily Dykeman, I'd give him the air if he ever came around again. It's too bad I lost that number."

"Lily Dykeman, huh? And you lost her telephone number?"

"A woman can't keep everything on her mind, mister. But I remember she said she worked at the Acme barber shop in the thirty-three hundred block on Broadway. She told me to tell Price to telephone her there when he came back."

That was all I got out of the place. But it was something. If this Lily Dykeman was Price's girl, she ought to know something about him.

I taxied up to Thirty-third and Broadway, paid off the cab and looked for the Acme barber shop. In the basement of a loft building I found it, a four-chair, second-rate shop with a mustached Greek at the cash register and only one woman in the place.

At the back a peroxide blonde at a manicure table was giving the works to a sallow-faced young man.

The Greek rolled a welcoming eye; the barber at the first chair waited expectantly, and I said, "Manicure."

So they let me alone until the sallow-face went away from the manicure table. I took his place while the cash register rang. The girl laughed at some sally from the customer and then swished back and sat down across the table.

"Manicure?" she asked coyly.

"I guess so."

AS SHE PUT her instruments in order she handed me a couple of easy looks from under high-arched eyebrows plucked thin. "You're a new customer, aren't you?"

"Not only to you, but to manicures, kid," I said, shoving out a handful of fingers. "See if you can make anything out of these nails and maybe I'll be back."

She smiled, smooth and bright, and we took a few seconds off to size each other up. She was a neat little worker at that.

"You'll be back then," she promised. "I always treat my customers right."

I'll bet she would have paid cash money for a good natural blush under the rouge. Blushes probably came hard to her these days. Sure she was passable; but mauling strange hands all day long hadn't softened her any. The cut-rate beauty parlors get her type by the thousands, turning 'em out in platoons modeled after this movie actress and that.

But she could handle a nail file like nobody's business and keep her mouth going at the same time. She had a smooth, fast line and she turned it on, eyebrows, chatter and tinkling laugh.

"Do you live here in town?" she chattered as she worked.

"Do I look it?"

That rated me a laugh. "You never can tell from a gent'mun's hands," she gave me. "We get lots of strangers in this district. Just yesterday I did the nails of a man from Sioux City. He said it was in Iowa."

"It was the last time I was there."

Thin brows arched and she turned the smile on. "Don't tell me you're from Sioux City too. There can't be this many nice men in one town away out there."

"You'd be surprised, sister. By the way, what do you hear from Price?"

The end of her file took a chunk of cuticle right out of my left forefinger as she jumped. That blonde looked as if she'd seen a ghost. First she got pale, then she got red.

"What do you know about Eddie?" she demanded. All idea of manicuring was gone for the moment.

"Me? What should I know about Eddie? We're old

friends is all. Didn't he ever tell you about Mike? Mike Harris, he used to live with?"

She snapped it back. "He never did! I guess there's a lot of things I never knew about Eddie. Did he tell you about me?"

"I'm here," I grinned at her.

That nailed her right. She stared for a moment and then asked hurriedly: "What did he say?"

"All sorts of things."

"Not so good, were they?" she said snappishly. "I thought so! That would be just like that dirty double-crosser. I always knew Eddie had that in him."

She had feelings on her mind. I teased 'em along.

"So Eddie double-crossed you too? I suppose you had to get it sooner or later. Where is he?"

She took a vicious slash at my fingernail with the file. "I wish I knew," she assured me. "I've got a few things to say to that chiseler that will make his head ring! If he thinks he can stand me up like he did, he'll find out better when I see him!"

"I see you've really met Eddie," I chuckled. "He's neat when he gets going, eh? How did he take you?"

THAT ALMOST BROUGHT her out of the chair.

"I was a sucker!" she said, close to tears. "I shoulda known better, but I got soft over that smile of his. Tossed aside two steadies I had.

"And then, after rushin' me steady for months, what does Eddie do but stand me up cold. Never a word out of him for six days, and me too proud to call him up and see what was the matter. I told the girls I room with that he was sick."

"Maybe he was."

"Sick!" Lily Dykeman says through her teeth—and did she have a hate on! "He was chasing around with a platinum blond hussy he had picked up somewhere! Ethel, my best girl friend, who dances in the chorus at the Club Renee, spotted 'em at a table one night last week."

"Maybe," says I, "it was an old friend of Eddie's. You know how it is; a fellow's got to be polite, even if they are platinum blondes packing everything."

She sawed down hard on my next nail. Her old lady may have named her Lily, but she was poison right then.

"If Eddie ever tries to hand me that line I'll claw his eyes out! Two weeks ago he never knew that hussy was alive! Ethel knows all about her. Dot Lancaster, she calls herself, and she's helped throw more money away than Eddie'll ever see in a lifetime!"

I had come expecting some fast evading, but if Lily wasn't telling the truth I had no business working for the Blaine Agency. She didn't know about the money Eddie was supposed to have hooked.

It looked like Eddie was a fast worker all around. As soon as he got his chunk of copper he grabbed himself a big time spender. But if Eddie was tooling around town with a high-stepping platinum blonde it wasn't going to be hard to put a hand on him.

I egged Lily on, keeping an eye peeled so I could snatch my hand back if her feelings took another surge.

"Maybe Eddie has got more money than you know about," I suggested.

That fell flat.

"Where'd he get it?" she asked scornfully. "I know what

he's been making: He didn't have over two hundred saved an' there wasn't a relative that could die and leave him any. I've lain awake nights wondering where he got the money to run around with a woman who used to be the sweetie of a spender like Tommy Verne."

I jumped then. The name came up so quick I wasn't set for it. Tommy Verne! Good Lord!

3

THE PLATINUM CLUE

LILY WAS TOO busy with her own troubles to notice what I did. I had time to think.

If I hadn't known about Sir Douglas MacClain's half million, I'd have lain awake nights myself wondering where small change like Eddie Price got off running around with an old girl of Tommy Verne's.

Granted Tommy Verne had ditched her; granted she wasn't in the money any more; she'd still have to take an awful slide before she got down to a penny-ante sport like Eddie Price.

Unless she knew something about more dough, or he had flashed some of it.

"Seems to me I've heard about Tommy Verne," I hedged; "Doesn't he own the Club Renee?"

"Sure he does! It's in the advertisements he runs in the papers. He's got more places like it, too. I can't understand what Eddie was doing in one of Verne's joints with an old girl of Verne's. It don't make sense, mister; it just don't."

She sighed. I found it in my heart—what little heart was left after years of this racket—to feel sorry for her. She had evidently fallen hard for Eddie and was having a rough time out of it.

So I said: "Don't let it get you. Maybe Eddie'll turn up with a good explanation. Sometimes they do."

She sniffed. "Usually they don't."

We both fell silent as she went on with my nails. I was thinking about Tommy Verne. I'd never met him, but I knew all about him. Most of the town did for that matter.

Tommy had started with one little speakeasy back in the early twenties. Before the easy money went out he had run that one dive into a sweet chain of hotsy-totsy joints that put him up into important money.

Most everybody knew Tommy Verne. He was easy to know. But when booze got legal and the deal changed, Tommy's speaks didn't do so well!

He blossomed out with an idea that looked like a wow at first; took over all the old Broadway theaters he could find, ripped out the seats, put in tables, hired some cheap vaudeville acts and gave the customers the whole works for the price of a cheap dinner, with dancing on the stage tossed in free when the acts weren't doing their stuff.

Bad booze and good food had given Tommy a bankroll. Good booze and ordinary food was taking the bankroll away. Not so many people knew that. But I heard a few asides about it. The overhead was fierce and the take not so good.

Now one of Tommy's old girls—he'd had plenty in the last ten years—was chasing with Eddie Price right under Verne's nose. Maybe it was just chance, but it didn't look right.

I fired another question at Lily. "Did you ever meet Eddie's friend, Colonel Humphries?"

"Who?"

"Humphries; Colonel Humphries."

"I not only never met, but I never heard of him."

I gave her the colonel in my own words as he had been described to me by Sir Douglas MacClain.

"He's about fifty-five, I guess. Sort of a tall, chesty man, with reddish cheeks and a short graying beard. Eyeglasses with a heavy black ribbon. Looks like a million dollars and talks like two million. Dignified all the time. Partly bald. Might be an old deacon at the corner church."

"I don't get you," says Lily, wrinkling her forehead. "Why would Eddie be chasing around with a dope like that? He never went in for no friends like that. You're springing something new on me, mister. Or is it a gag?"

"Straight stuff. Eddie had a friend here in town like that."

She sighed.

"I'm beginnin' to believe Eddie might have done anything while he was running around with me. And I thought I knew everything about him."

She fell silent again and finished my nails. I paid her before I left the table, adding a half dollar tip from the Blaine Agency. She'd earned it although she didn't know it.

"You're a gentleman even if you are a friend of Eddie's," she told me. "I don't suppose you'll be seeing him."

"If I do, I'll send him around."

SO FAR I hadn't gotten close to Eddie and the bonds. But I was getting warm. This Dot Lancaster knew where Eddie was. I had to find her.

And I went about that as cheerfully as I ever made a move. My pet peeve was a double-crossing crook who eased into someone's trust and made his snatch while eyes were off him. A baby could get dough that way. It doesn't take brains to loot a man who trusts you, only a cheap, shabby brand of crookedness.

Colonel Humphries had me wondering too. Sir Douglas MacClain had been brief about him. Too brief. Hadn't seemed to want to go into the business relations he'd had with the colonel.

Maybe it had been better he didn't. Despite the trust fund which had been put under Sir Douglas's care, and all his shouting about the family honor, I had a growing hunch Sir Douglas leaned a bit on the shady side himself.

And though Sir Douglas was paying the Blaine Agency, and so my salary and expenses, I made up my mind to toss him to the dogs if I got a chance to uncover anything on him. For next to a man like Price, I had no use for a slippery crook who went around dripping sanctimonious honesty.

The easiest way to get track of Dot Lancaster was through Tommy Verne, himself. Tommy was posted on a lot that went on. And that dinner with Price right under Verne's nose looked cockeyed to me as I thought about it.

I walked up Broadway toward Times Square, wondering how to get a line on La Lancaster. She wouldn't talk of course. Broadway-wise, suspicious, she'd give any questions a loud yodel and cover up like a ham fighter coasting for the last bell.

Con Craddock popped into my mind. He was the perfect answer, and about this time in the afternoon he was due to be stirring somewhere between Herald Square and the Circle.

Maybe you're one of the herd who shelled out two

cents every day to see what Con had spilled in his column: *Broadway and Why.* I did myself now and then.

It took me an hour and a half to pick up Con's trail and run it down. I found him near Forty-sixth Street, at the back of a bar, eyeing the foam on a small beer and listening as the barkeep told him something in an undertone. As I breasted the bar, Con smiled, shook his head, said something in return.

"Gimme a beer," I called, and as the barkeep tore himself away, got out a surprised: "Hello, Con! Still digging the dirt?"

Con straightened his lanky shoulders and slid his beer along the bar to me. He was grinning that twisted open grin that made him friends everywhere.

"Dad gum my whiskers, ef hit hain't Mike Harris," says Con, grabbing my fist. "I was thinking about you the other day. What's new?"

"I knew it," I sighed, reaching for my beer. "If you're wondering how much of your column I can write today, you'd better unload at the next stop. Nothing's new. The same old sausage everywhere."

"It'll always stand spicing up to a different flavor," Con said, grinning. "Take your beer slow, Michael, my boy, and see if you can stir up a couple of lines worth printing. I'm short today and the column calleth, the column calleth."

The barkeep grinned at us.

"I thought I had something Mr. Craddock could use, but he knew it yesterday, almost before it happened."

"So why bother to tell him anything?" I said, and buried my snoot in the beer and wondered if Con would go along with me on this Lancaster angle.

I COULD TELL him all, of course—and maybe he'd turn me down. I needed him my way. We finished our beers, Con yawned, glanced at his wrist watch. "Got to be going. Lots to do."

I walked to the door with him.

"Maybe I've got something that'll turn into a nice little story," I mused. "Can't give it to you now. Later, maybe, when I have some more of it."

We were outside by then. Con chuckled as he took my arm and steered me over to a quiet spot between two show windows.

"I thought you had something up your sleeve, Mike. Let's have it. I won't print until you pass the word."

"Nix. If anything goes wrong and there's a leak I don't want you to feel uncomfortable. This is hot. Red hot."

Con looked hopeful. "Isn't there any part of it I could tease 'em with, Mike?"

"Not a thing. In fact, I don't know whether you'll ever be able to print much of it. The Blaine Agency was called in to dodge publicity. But the way things are shaping up, maybe it can't be helped. I'll have to see how it turns out"

"It won't be the first time I've done a little spade work to get a good story growing," Con assured me cheerfully. "What do I do?"

"Ever hear of a girl named Dot Lancaster?"

Con handed it back instantly. "Tommy Verne was nuts over her last year. A platinum blonde with the sweetest pair of underpins I've seen in a long time."

"What's she doing now?"

"Search me. I see her around now and then. She doesn't

seem to be working or chiseling. Looks to me like she's still in the money."

"She going with Verne any?"

"Not that I know of, and that's a funny thing," Con said thoughtfully. "Never struck me before. Tommy Verne hasn't had a new girl since he laid off Lancaster. You see him around now and then with one, but nothing serious about it. Funny. He used to go for them heavy. Maybe he's working too hard these days. I'll send up a trial balloon in the column and see what it brings out."

"Why not drop around and pump Verne a little?" I suggested. "Better still, take me along, as the visiting country cousin getting an eyeful of Broadway? You can ask Tommy where La Lancaster lives, what she's doing, who she's chasing with and all that. Just casually."

Con gave me a thoughtful look. "Something wrong with Dot Lancaster, eh?"

"How should I know? If I start guessing, I'll be talking. Take me in with you and see what you can find out from Verne."

Con chuckled. "What a gag! Sure, come along. But keep your lines straight. If you're going to be a country cousin, be one. No 'dese' and 'dem.' Tommy'll be wise like a shot."

4

THE OPEN DRAWER

TOMMY VERNE'S OFFICE was upstairs over the Club Renee. His bankroll might have been getting slim but you'd never know it from the surroundings. Broadway from spats to sleek hair, Tommy had surrounded himself with a lather of flash and glitter; paneled walls, thick rugs, and modern furniture.

The small waiting room might have been a Park Avenue reception room. But the brunette dream who took Con's name almost fell over herself getting in with it. Con rated high, with the publicity he could give.

As the brunette showed us in, Tommy Verne himself was posed behind an acre of flat desk which was a masterpiece of rubbed, polished mahogany. Yeah, posed—with a pen in one hand and a thin cheek resting on the other fist in attitude of deep thought.

Con laughed in that booming, jovial way he had. "Never mind the act, Tommy," he said. "I've seen it before. Be yourself. Meet the country cousin, Wilbur Craddock, who's getting an eyeful of the Main Stem. Wilbur, this is the great Tommy Verne in the flesh. Not quite as good as he sometimes thinks he is, but he's put over plenty just the same."

Verne came around the desk and shook hands with me. I'm short and red-headed. Verne wasn't any taller, but his hair was black, combed down smooth and careful.

"Glad to know you, Wilbur," he said with easy familiarity. "Any relation of Con's is a friend of mine. Don't believe half what he tells you and a quarter he prints. This your first trip to New York?"

"Kind of," says I bashfully. Sure—bashfully. "Some place, isn't it? I've read about these theaters you've made over, Mr. Verne. It sounded like a slick idea and I'm sure happy to know you."

Lousy acting I know, but Pittsburgh was out west for Verne. It was gag enough for him to be showing off before an admiring yokel.

"Sit down, boys," he said, drawing two chairs to the back of the desk, close on either side of his own chair. "Smoke?" he said to me, flipping open an enameled humidor lined with cedar that stood on his desk.

"Thanks," I said, grabbing myself two cigars. They were good ones, too. I unwrapped one and lit it.

Con took one also. We all sat down, lighted up, and Con started batting hot air. "How's business?" he asked.

"Swell," says Verne, leaning back and blowing a big smoke ring. "I'm cleaning up."

"You're a wizard," Con told him heartily.

Verne came back modestly. "Not exactly that."

"Plenty wizard to be grabbing off a profit with so many tables empty all the time," Con said generously. He smiled knowingly. "Been sleeping well lately, Tommy?"

I'd noticed it. Verne's sallow face had a tired look. He was tailored, barbered and spruced up. He moved lively and spoke lively, but the zip didn't seem to go all the way through him.

Verne turned as if into a laugh. "Trying to gag me around to see my doctor, Con? I sleep like a top. And you must have looked in my places at the wrong times. We're doing a fast business. Tables filled every night. Don't go printing any bad cracks about it."

"Why should I?" said Con. "I don't kick a man when he's already going down. But don't try to kid me, Tommy. I don't fall for a flash."

VERNE'S LOOK WANDERED over to me. Con got the implication.

"Wilbur's a clam," he said. "And anyway, he'll be out of town in a day or so. He couldn't do you any harm if he wanted to."

Verne shrugged, grinned. "It doesn't matter how many full or empty tables I've got. The places are open for business. How about giving me a little publicity, Con?"

"Sure," Con agreed readily. "I can think of lots of easy things to say. I could use a good woman angle too. By the way, whatever happened to that platinum blonde you used to take around? She did an act for you. Let's see, her name was Lancaster, wasn't it? Dot Lancaster?"

Verne had been blowing another smoke ring. It broke up as his glance jerked quickly to Con. He jammed the cigar in his mouth, puffed deeply before he said anything; then his answer was elaborately casual. Just a shade too casual.

"That was her name—Dot Lancaster. Great kid. Too bad we weren't able to hit it off. I guess I'm a hard one to get along with. We had our differences and she walked out."

"She was pretty good," Con mused. "What's she doing now?"

Verne shrugged carelessly. "I see her around now and then. Don't know what she's doing."

"She's still in town then?"

"I don't know," Verne declared shortly. Some of the welcome had left his manner. "Why so interested inner?"

Con grinned happily.

"She'd make a swell item for the column. Get it? What Broadway did for one kid who had the looks and savvee. I'll see what I can dig up about her. Everything she's been doing since you two broke up."

Verne suddenly wasn't smiling as he stared at Con, and his face was hard.

"Lay off, Con!" he ordered harshly. "If you've got to hustle up a story like that, take someone beside Dot Lancaster!"

Con lifted his eyebrows. He didn't know what was behind our visit and probably didn't care, but this was the sort of thing that would nail his interest.

"Why not Dot Lancaster?" Con came back. "You've broken off with her, haven't you?"

"Sure," said Verne. "But you heard me. No publicity about her. I don't want it raked up."

His eyes were hard and ugly as he looked at Con and then around at me. Con's face was dead-pan.

I had to look dumb, but inside I felt good. I'd had a hunch and it was working out. A man didn't get all stirred up this way for old times sake; not over a little thing like Con Craddock making a few remarks in his column.

Con was puzzled himself. He could see there was more

to this than Verne was telling. But after a moment he grinned wryly.

"You're taking it too hard, Tommy. I don't see what's so poison about the idea. Plenty would fall over for a break like that. You just asked for some publicity yourself; and when I take you up on it, you start snapping. That's a hell of a way to do. I'll keep you in mind after this—I will not!"

Con was beginning to get mad about it.

Verne was a fast thinker. He'd said more than he wanted to, I guess. He grinned placatingly.

"It's just the way I feel, Con. No offense meant. If you want a story like that, I know a dozen dames that will make better copy!"

The telephone rang. Verne answered it, stopped smiling, snapped back. "I don't want to see him in here! Tell him to wait a minute and I'll be out!"

HE SET THE phone down and took out a leather key-holder, talking to us as he unlocked a desk drawer on my side.

"I've got to see a man out in front for a few minutes. Don't go. I want to talk to you some more about this, Con."

My chair was placed back far enough so I could look down in the drawer as Verne reached into it. I looked— and got a shock.

Placed at an angle in the drawer, where the man in the desk chair could look down and view it by merely opening the drawer a little, was a swell portrait of a platinum blonde who would knock your eye out. A dame any man would find easy on the eyes.

Before I saw the signature, I knew her. Dot Lancaster, of course; Dot Lancaster there in the drawer where Tommy Verne could look at her any minute, with none the wiser.

Over her signature she had written something and put a date. I didn't have a chance to read it.

Verne stood up with an envelope he had taken from the front part of the drawer.

"I'll be right back," he assured Con, and hurried out, closing the door behind him.

Con was sore.

"What's the matter with that guy?" he asked me. "Getting all hot over a little thing like that! Where does this Lancaster wench come in anyway?"

"Maybe I'll know more about it in a minute," I said, easing forward out of the chair.

Verne had left the drawer unlocked. I pulled it out and took a good eyeful of the picture. She had written: *To Tommy, with my undying love, Dot.* And dated the inscription.

Con said: "Hey, I didn't bring you in here to go through his desk! Lay off!"

"Take a gander at this," I urged.

It brought him out of his chair, where he could look down into the drawer. "I'll be damned!" Con said under his breath. "It's dated last week, isn't it? He's been giving us the run-around. Say, that telegram's signed Dot, too. What's in it?"

A carelessly folded telegram had been tossed in against the bottom of the picture. The signature was showing. "Dot" it said.

With Con Craddock urging me, I flipped the wire open and read it. I'd have done so anyway. The message was dated from Baltimore, two days before.

EVERYTHING HOTSY BUT NO GO HERE STOP
LEAVING TOMORROW STOP WILL TELEPHONE
LATER STOP ALL KINDS OF LOVE
DOT

I dropped that wire and tried to close the drawer as I heard the office door starting to open behind me.

5

SURPRISE ATTACK

IT WAS TOMMY Verne of course. He stepped into the office fast, like he had been suspicious all the time. The drawer wasn't closed. Con and I were there on our feet cold.

We couldn't even laugh it off. I tried to.

"I saw that picture when you opened the drawer, and I took another look at it," I said, grinning at Verne. "She sure is a swell looker, ain't she, Mr. Verne?"

And Con chimed in heartily: "If that's Dot Lancaster, she's even better looking than I remember her."

I don't think Tommy Verne heard us. He wasn't smiling as he slammed the door and jumped to the desk. For a moment I thought he had gone crazy as he elbowed me aside to get at the desk. His face looked that way, sallow, twisted, furious.

He yanked out the drawer, took one gander, and slammed it shut again. I hadn't had time to refold the telegram. He knew I'd read it, and if I ever saw murder on a man's face, it was there on Verne's as he turned to me.

"You! Damn you! What do you mean prying in my desk?"

"I told you."

And Con said: "Now, Tommy, don't take it that way. Wilbur was—"

"Shut up!" Verne yelled at him. "I thought there was something screwy about this visit, bringing a hick cousin in here to see me!"

I had stepped back. The next instant I wished I hadn't. Verne shoved his right hand under his coat. He was wearing a shoulder holster and gun. Police permit, I guess. And he meant to use the gun on me. He was crazy with anger. In his eyes was murder, nothing less.

If I ran, he'd get me in the back. I had a chance to beat the shot by jumping at him. Half an eyelash before I started he caught himself, pulled his hand out empty.

I poised on my toes, ready for anything.

For a moment Verne stood there, shaking like a leaf. I was doing a little delayed shaking myself. I'd been too close to death for comfort. I knew, better than Verne himself perhaps, that if I'd rushed him he'd have drawn and shot.

We were all of us in a spell. I found my voice first.

"I guess we'd better go, Con. Too bad Mr. Verne took offense this way!"

Con stepped warily around the desk with his eyes on Verne. Con was white, silent; talk wouldn't help and all he wanted to do was get out of there.

We were almost to the door when Verne found his voice.

"If you ever talk about this, or print a word on Dot Lancaster, I'll kill you like a yellow dog, Craddock!" he warned huskily, and then he added as an anti-climax: "Dot's trying to break away from this Broadway racket and I'm helping her."

Con didn't answer. We went out past the gorgeous brunette, walked downstairs and out on Broadway without a word. Then, as we mingled with the crowd, Con spoke wonderingly.

"I was afraid back there, Mike. Afraid as hell. He was all set to rub you out, and me next, I guess."

"It looked that way, didn't it? I didn't mean to get you in a mess like that, Con." And I hadn't.

"I know. Partly my fault. We should have stayed out of that drawer. Come in Danny's and have a drink. I'm weak."

THE PLACE WAS crowded. We found a vacant booth clear at the back. Con ordered whisky straight and I ordered black coffee and cognac. When the waiter was gone Con leaned on his elbows and looked at me.

"What the hell have you got me mixed up in, Mike?" he demanded.

I owed it to Con by then, so I gave him the layout quick and short; what I knew, what I suspected—what I didn't know and what I'd like to know.

Con downed his whisky when it came and listened intently to the end, then drew a deep breath.

"So that's what we were digging into?" he said slowly. "If Verne is mixed in that, not knowing what we might be after, no wonder he was jumpy. Hell—half a million! That's real money. It's worth trying to cover up. If Verne has any part of it, he's deeper than I ever figured; although I always knew he had plenty of contacts."

I said: "He's covering something up. What did he want to lie about the girl for? What's the idea of publicly breaking off from her last year, and still being thick with her on the side?"

"How should I know?" Con reached over and took my cognac. "I'm still jittery," he confessed. "I didn't like the look in Verne's eye when we left. What are you going to do now?"

"Back to the office and think it over. First I want to know where Lancaster is. What was she doing down in Baltimore, and where did she go to the next morning?"

"I'll look around and see if anyone's seen her yesterday or today," Con said. "I've got to run along now. Never mind the check—I'll get it."

Fat, beaming Danny was at his post behind the cash register. He recognized me. While I passed remarks with Danny, Con Craddock went on out ahead of me. When I followed, Con was already heading toward Forty-second Street. Walking fast, Con was, bending his head to hear something a man beside him was saying.

I thought too slow, for just as the answer came to me I felt a nudge in my side. A curt voice warned me:

"Follow your sidekick if you want to keep healthy!"

I had the answer then, but what good did it do me? Con Craddock was walking off that way because a gun was against his side—and so was I.

6

A DOUBLE SNATCH

MY MAN HAD a round, flabby face and a pair of bulging eyes suggesting high blood pressure. A couple of inches taller than me, nothing about him stood out in the crowd through which we jostled. He was smiling slightly—smiling while his right hand, down in his coat pocket, poked a hard gun muzzle against my left side.

I wasn't afraid—yet. Not like I'd been when Tommy Verne went for his gun. If quick shooting was planned it could have been done back there in front of Danny's just as well.

But I didn't feel so good over what might be coming. Con Craddock had been right about that bad look in Verne's eye. Verne was behind this, of course, and that might mean anything.

I said: "What does Verne think he's doing?"

"I'll do the talkin'!" I was warned sharply. The voice was high-pitched, almost feminine. But there was nothing feminine about the way he was handling me.

Ever walk and jostle through a crowd while a gun jabs your side? People look at you but they don't really see you. You wonder what they'd do if they knew what was happening right under their noses. But you don't try to find out.

Smack among the crowd, you're more alone than you'd be on the desert.

Maybe, I thought, Con Craddock was thinking the same thing as he walked there ahead of us. Times Square was just beginning to glint and glitter with the first night lights. It was the same old square, and I wondered if I'd ever see it again as Con and his companion turned off to the right. In turn I was neatly steered around the same corner by the gun at my side.

We were just in time to see Con and his man enter a taxi and roll off without waiting for us. I didn't get the number, for my man jostled me over to the curb, hailed another cab, opened the door for me and grunted:

"Get in."

I got. I wasn't ready for a bullet in the back. Not yet. As I sat down my man ducked in after me—and I flopped back on the seat and kicked him in the jaw.

He must have thought the pavement had smacked him—if he thought at all. Lurching over against the front seat, he sprawled across my feet.

"What tha' hell!" the driver exclaimed, and I knew he wasn't working for Tommy Verne.

At the moment the sidewalk was clear outside the taxi door. We had the thing to ourselves.

"Take it easy!" I told the hackie quickly, as I reached over and closed the door. "Drive to the precinct station."

We started off and I hauled my man up on the seat and went into his pocket after the gun. It was an off-brand thirty-two automatic, Spanish manufacture by the looks of it, just right for pocket size, and worth plenty of trouble under the gun law if he didn't have a permit. Somehow I had an idea he didn't have a permit.

He'd been knocked out clean and as the taxi weaved through the traffic he came out of it.

"Wh-wha's matter?" he mumbled, lifting his head. Groggy amazement was plastered over his pudgy face.

"It's a sad story, you mug!" I said, goading him in the side with his own gun. "You asked for it an' you got it. It's a pinch now and if you know a shyster lawyer who can get you out of this, you're a better hoodlum than you look to me."

I THOUGHT HE was going to faint. It must be a shock to nail your man and suddenly to wake up to hear you're pinched instead.

He sat, licking his lips, scowling as he tried to think and finally the hack swung in to the curb and stopped.

"Pay the driver, mug," I told my prisoner.

Looking dazed he obeyed from where he sat, and followed me out into the street through the door on my side. Loud enough for the driver to hear, I said: "All right, now get on in the station!"

We walked behind the hack and made the sidewalk as it drove off. Moving slow, we were just about starting to enter the station when it turned the corner.

"Never mind," I said abruptly. "We're not going inside right now."

I walked him back along the sidewalk until I got another taxi, and loaded him in, careful he didn't try any tricks on me. But he still was too dazed to have any such ideas.

"Where we going?" he asked.

"Sightseeing," said I. "But first, where did my friend go?"

His jaw set stubbornly. He made no reply.

"Have it your way," I said cheerfully, and left him to wonder what his way would get him as we rolled across town, and finally took the elevator up to Thompson's office.

Thompson was still on the job, dictating to his secretary, while Trixie Meehan perched on one corner of the desk swinging her feet.

Thompson broke off, stared past his cigar, and then jumped to his feet as I shoved my prisoner down in a chair and waved the thirty-two under his nose.

"Home is the hunter, home from the sea," Trixie misquoted sarcastically. "Watch that gun, Mike. You're too clumsy to be juggling dangerous weapons that way."

Thompson came around the desk, demanding: "What's the idea, Mike? Who is he?"

"Haven't time to find out. But his name'll be mud if he doesn't loosen up and bare all."

The sign on the door had tipped the prisoner off that he was in the Blaine Agency offices and made it plain I wasn't a city dick. His assurance came back with a bang. He started to get up, protesting in that high-pitched voice.

"So you ain't a city dick after all? That was a fake pinch then! Lemme out of—"

I shoved my palm in his face and sat him down hard again.

"I thought you'd yell that," I said. "What if I'm not a city dick? Where's your permit to carry this gun?"

A smooth grin broke over his pudgy face.

"What gun?" he asked. "I ain't got a gun. I don't know nothing about a gun. I never carry 'em myself. It's against the law."

Trixie chortled.

He gave her a dirty look.

"If anyone in this dump figures to frame me, it won't go over, see?" he warned. "I ain't a cluck."

"Turn it off," I said wearily. "You'll begin believing it yourself. The Sullivan law isn't the only thing you've got to worry about. What happened to Con Craddock? Where is he?"

Feeling his sore jaw, he scowled at me. "I don't know anything," he denied. "An' I could go on the griddle at Centre Street and still not know. Get it? I don't know."

I BELIEVED HIM, which didn't make me such a sucker at that. I'd been thinking all along it was queer that Con had been taken off alone, ahead of me.

"This fellow's partner kidnapped Con Craddock," I said to Thompson. "This man stuck a gun in my side and forced me into a taxi. Maybe he doesn't know where Con went, but he knows who wanted Con and me. And so do I for that matter."

He sneered at me.

"Who?" Thompson questioned me sharply.

"I could have tossed this one to the coppers after I took his gun away from him, but I brought him here to see what he knew before he faced a rap for kidnapping," I said. "There's plenty of publicity in this."

"Hmmmmm," says Thompson thoughtfully. He was thinking, I knew, about Sir Douglas MacClain's ban against publicity. "You did right to bring him here, Mike, if you think he knows anything. Uh, I'm a bit vague about this Craddock matter."

"Get one of the boys to watch this."

Thompson called in Shorty Simms, who stood six feet three and was built like a Dutch weight lifter. Thompson and Trixie went into the next room with me. I brought them up to date on the MacClain case.

"Maybe Con is dead now," I finished. "If he's not, a little delay may give him more gray hairs, but it won't hurt him."

Trixie mused: "If he's dead, that would be a typical Craddock ending, wouldn't it? A bang of excitement, right out of the Broadway lights. He'd get a kick out of that."

"And I get a pain out of such cracks," I said. "You've got about as much heart as a lithographed bowl of fruit."

"Uts-nay!" said Trixie.

I let it ride at that. You couldn't argue with that handful of hell on wheels. Little Trixie's blond and innocent looks would make you drop your guard—and then she'd cut you to pieces with the razor edge of her tongue.

To look at Trixie Meehan you'd think she needed a guardian—and there wasn't a smarter, cooler, more dangerous operative on the whole great payroll of the Blaine organization. Which was okay except that Trixie was at my throat every chance she got.

Thompson was quiet, thoughtful.

"Tommy Verne, huh?" he said, dragging on his cigar. "Funny. Not much sense to it. Trixie has just come in with a report on this Colonel Humphries. He has been living at the Waldorf for six weeks. He checked out day before yesterday and took his trunk with him. Left no forwarding address."

"Which looks," says I, "as if he was all set for the snatch and run. What else did you find out about him, Trixie?—if you have to be tangled in this case."

"I hate rubbing elbows with you on it worse than you do, Ape," Trixie says pleasantly. "Thompson will tell you I tried to beg off when I heard you were on it."

"Lay off this fighting, you two!" Thompson squalled angrily. "I get a chill every time I have to team you two on a case. I never know when you're going to be at each other's throats. Miss Meehan found out that Humphries was supposed to be a promoter; that's all she could pick up."

"And did he promote himself something this time?" Trixie murmured. "Half a million! I shudder to think what I'd be capable of for that much money. My idea is he was stringing MacClain along for the chance of an 'in' with this Eddie Price."

AND I SAID: "I think the whole thing is screwy and off the level somewhere. Including Sir Douglas MacClain. I don't like his cut. Whoever handed MacClain a two million trust fund was plain dopey."

Thompson gave me a queer look. "We're not investigating MacClain or his business affairs," he reminded.

"His money's good even if he happens to be a crook, eh?"

And Thompson came back irritably: "Dammit, why bring that up? You know the Blaine Agency doesn't take cases that are shady. We'd pass up a hundred grand fee if we thought it wasn't on the level. But here's a Knight of the British Empire, with nothing against him as far as we know, who asks us to recover property which has been stolen from him. It's an open and shut proposition, with a good cash fee, and there's nothing we can do but crack the case as fast as we can."

"And get Con Craddock back—and keep the wolves away from Mike Harris," I said. "My number is still up.

Tommy Verne must be wanting me pretty bad. Sweet, isn't it? MacClain's money is blowing up a bigger and better mess of trouble every hour or so."

"And what," says Trixie, "has that grandiose brain of yours decided to do about it, if any?"

"Send a couple of men to cover Tommy Verne," I said. "They probably won't pick him up, but if they do, I want to see him. He knows where Con Craddock is, and now that I've walked off with his man, he'll be careful of Con. Chances are that he knows who I am already, from Danny. Trixie, call Tommy Verne's office and see if he's in."

Trixie did, and got no sale.

"Try the Club Renee downstairs."

Trixie hung up a second time. "Mr. Verne hasn't been in this evening. They don't know where he is, or where he might be found."

"So far, so good. And the next thing," I decided, "is to get a line on this Dot Lancaster. She's been in town here, mixing with the public, getting all the money she needs from Tommy Verne, of course. She hasn't been living in one room, either. Not with that setup. And she'd have a telephone, which should be listed in the book; and I'm a dope for not having thought of it before."

"Hear, hear!" Trixie applauded as I opened the telephone directory.

There it was, Seventy-eighth Street, west.

"Telephone her," I said to Trixie. "If she answers, stall the wrong number."

Trixie made the call, got no reply.

"We're off," says I to Thompson. "See what you can get out of that mug in the other room. I doubt if he'll talk.

He knows we can't do anything much to him, but keep him here anyway. I want Verne guessing as to what has happened to his man, and what I'm doing."

But it was me who was wondering where Verne was and what he was doing as I hurried to my locker, strapped on my shoulder gun, and dropped a ring of keys in my pocket. On second thought I took a small flashlight too.

IT WAS AFTER eight o'clock when I paid off another taxi driver and walked toward Dot Lancaster's apartment with Trixie Meehan. Only the address in the telephone book was not an apartment.

It was a house; a two story house, with a stone front, sandwiched in between two apartment buildings. The heavily curtained front windows showed faint light inside.

We walked slowly past. Trixie made a cynical remark.

"The lady has been doing well by herself, hasn't she?"

"I guess she can afford it, if she's tied in so thick with Tommy Verne. What I want to know, who's in there?"

"The gal herself, probably."

"Why didn't she answer your telephone call?"

"Maybe she's come in since I called. Or maybe," Trixie suggested, "someone else lives here too."

"In that case we certainly will have a run of luck. If La Lancaster isn't here, and a friend is, you're the bosom pal who just got in from Boston and wants to see 'dear Dot' At least you want to know where she is and how you can get in touch with her."

"And if it's Lancaster herself?"

"Give me the high sign and I'll come in and talk to her."

"Suppose her gentleman friend is there?"

"I'll come in anyway, I want to see him as bad as I do

Lancaster. I've got a gun this time and I'll find out quick what he did with Con Craddock—and maybe why."

Trixie caught my arm, serious for once.

"I don't like this gun business, Mike. If Verne is desperate for any reason, he might shoot you; or you might have to shoot him."

"I can think of less pleasant things to do. I've had all of that bird I want. He's gunning for me now, and we might as well have it out. I'll wait here on the sidewalk."

"Well, here I go for better or worse," said Trixie, and she walked up to the front door, opened it and stepped inside.

The first double doors gave into a sheltered entrance way. Enough glow came from the curb lights to show Trixie's shadowy head and shoulders waiting at an inner door.

Someone answered Trixie's ring. I saw her move on inside and vanish. Standing there on the sidewalk I wondered who it was, why I hadn't seen a light, how she was carrying it off.

Ten seconds perhaps I stood there and then I thought I heard a faint, choking cry.

Just once.

Perhaps I was mistaken. But I couldn't afford to be uncertain. Loosening the gun under my arm, I went up the steps on my toes. The front doors opened easily enough. As they closed behind me, cutting off most of the outside noises, I heard a dull muffled thump in the house as if a chair had been kicked over. That was enough.

7

HANDS OF A MURDERER

THE INNER DOOR had no glass. I grabbed the knob, found the door locked, on a spring lock inside, evidently.

The house was old. That spring lock was probably attached to the inside by screws. It wouldn't be too strong. This was one of the times when I wished fate had given me six feet and a half, and two hundred odd pounds of weight. I needed it all to get through that door quickly.

I was afraid again, afraid for Trixie Meehan; game little Trixie, who would tackle a wildcat with her bare hands, and who was in God knew what trouble inside. I hit that door with every ounce of my weight back of my shoulder.

The door shivered, cracked loudly. I drew back and hit it again. This time screws came out of wood with a loud tearing sound. The door flew open. I staggered on through, drawing my gun.

"Trixie!" I yelled.

But Trixie didn't answer.

The flashlight showed stairs going up, and a door on my left opening into the lighted room. Only the room wasn't lighted when I kicked open the door and entered. In those short moments since I had left the sidewalk, someone had turned out the light.

The flash beam swinging to the back of the room stopped on heavy curtains parted slightly in the middle and trembling faintly as if someone had just whisked through them. Just as I started for those curtains, a faint gasp sounded on the floor before me. The light beam dropped and came to rest on Trixie Meehan lying crumbled, moving feebly, gasping weakly.

"Trixie!" I gulped.

I could hardly get it out as I went to my knees beside her. Something was the matter with my throat—and my heart. In that moment I didn't give a damn who had gone through the curtains. Not with Trixie crumpled there.

Her face was pale, but her hands were moving and she was trying to push herself up to a sitting position. I helped her, my arm tight around her shoulder. And Trixie gasped, drew a deep shuddery breath. When she spoke I hardly knew her voice, so small, so thick and labored was it.

"I—I'll be all right, Mike. He choked me. I think he was trying to kill me."

"Who was it?"

"I don't know," Trixie whispered. "He ran out the back of the room. See if you can catch him."

That was Trixie Meehan, the Blaine Agency's crack woman operative, half dead but still on the job.

I went through the curtains with my finger on the automatic trigger, ready to shoot at sight. I found nothing. In the kitchen I found the answer. The back door stood ajar an inch or so. Someone had made a hurried exit out this way.

A key was still in the door lock. Using my handkerchief to avoid fingerprints, I closed the door, locked it, hurried back to Trixie. She had gotten up, collapsed in a chair. My light on her face found a smile. Yes, Trixie was smiling after that close shave.

"What happened?" I asked gruffly.

"I rang the buzzer. Someone opened the door. It was dark. I couldn't see who it was, and he didn't speak. Before I could say anything, he caught me by the throat. I didn't have a chance. I tried to get the gun out of my handbag and he tore the bag out of my hand. There it is on the floor by the door. I scratched and clawed and tried to scream; and he just held me and choked harder. He dragged me in here. We staggered around and then everything began to whirl and I almost fainted."

"Didn't you see him?"

"No. The light in the room was out."

STANDING OVER HER, I put the light on her throat, and swore under my breath at the dark finger bruises on the white skin. At one spot the skin had been broken and a tiny smear of blood showed.

Trixie fingered her throat very gingerly.

"I'll have a sore neck tomorrow, Mike. It feels as if he punched a hole right into my windpipe. He was wearing some sort of a ring, with a large rough setting. It got twisted around and pressed into my neck. I think I tore the skin on the back of his hand with my fingernails. I was frantic."

Savagely I said: "I wish you could have gotten your gun out and killed him! Anyway he's gone; lammed out the back door. I wonder if it was Tommy Verne."

"I don't think so. I've seen Tommy Verne. This man seemed larger. Anyway, I don't think Verne would have caught me by the throat. He would have turned on the light to see who I was—or at least not answered my ring. This man evidently didn't have a right to be in here."

"Queer," I muttered. "Damn queer. In fact, the more that happens in this case, the queerer it gets. I'm going to turn on the light and look around."

The light button was beside the hall doorway. It turned on a single floor lamp across the room. Turning to Trixie I found her staring toward the front of the room. She pointed.

"Look, Mike!" Trixie gulped.

I did—and blinked, and said: *"Good God!"*

A big overstuffed divan occupied most of the front end of that living room. On the floor at its left end, half hidden behind the divan, was the grotesque huddle of a woman.

She evidently had been crowded there in a hurried effort to get her out of the way. I bent over her and she did not move. Her head was twisted at a tortuous angle. The eyes were wide and staring. She was dead, of course.

Trixie shivered.

Trixie whispered. "Who is that?"

"Not Dot Lancaster," I said.

This woman had black hair, combed smoothly back into a knot at the rear. She was somewhere in her early thirties. From the plain black dress she wore, I made a hurried guess.

"She must be the maid." Looking closely, using my flashlight, I suddenly added: "There wasn't anyone to stop him when he grabbed *her* throat. His fingerprints are here on the neck."

"God help her," said Trixie. "How terrified she must have been. I know. Are—are you going to call the police, Mike?"

"Not unless I have to. It's too much of a mess already."

I didn't touch the body. It wouldn't help the woman. Examination was up to the police. Too well Trixie and I knew how she had met her death. But why? I couldn't get that out of my mind. Why had she been killed wantonly, coldbloodedly?

I could think of no sensible answer, so I turned away to look about the room.

Against the side wall was a small formal fireplace under a carved wooden mantel. I saw the letters on the end of the mantel before Trixie did. None had been opened. Taking them gingerly in my handkerchief, I leafed through them. Nine letters and two telegrams. The telegrams were on top. Evidently delivered last, they had been placed on top of the other mail by the maid.

Letters and wires were addressed to Miss Dorothy Lancaster. Looking through the transparent part of the telegram envelopes, I saw that both wires had been sent from Buffalo the day before.

I opened them.

SO HELP ME I didn't expect what I found. After I had read the wires twice, I still couldn't make much sense out of them. The first one, sent at eleven-eight in the morning, said:

> WAITING ANXIOUSLY STOP HAVE YOU LEFT
> STOP LOVE
> > EDDIE

The second one had been sent at four-twenty-four in the afternoon.

IF YOU ARE THERE WHY DON'T YOU ANSWER
MY WIRE STOP NEITHER THE COLONEL OR I
CAN UNDERSTAND DELAY STOP WERE YOU
KIDDING ME ABOUT EVERYTHING STOP IF
YOU HAVE LEFT BY NOW YOU WILL BE HERE
IN THE MORNING STOP IF YOURE NOT HERE
BY MORNING I'LL KNOW YOU LIED TO ME AND
I'LL COME BACK STOP ALL KINDS OF
LOVE FORLORNLY
EDDIE

"It's all rather foggy, isn't it?" Trixie said. "Both wires sound as if he was expecting Lancaster in Buffalo. He and this Colonel Humphries."

"That's plain enough. Price seems to be goofy about the woman. And yet she belongs to Tommy Verne. While Price is in Buffalo waiting for her, evidently by prearrangement, she is in Baltimore wiring her love to Verne."

"Didn't you say, Mike, she wired Verne from Baltimore she was leaving in the morning?"

"Yes. But hardly for Buffalo—unless she was double-crossing Verne too. If she intended to go to Buffalo, why did she go to Baltimore first?"

"I wonder if Eddie Price returned as he threatened in this last wire," Trixie said thoughtfully, handing the telegrams back to me.

"God knows." Then a thought struck me. "If he came back, and came here to the house…."

We both looked at the body beside the divan.

Trixie said: "According to those wires he was head over

heels in love. A man disappointed in love is apt to do strange things."

"Exactly. Even murder. But why kill the maid?"

"You wouldn't know anything about it," Trixie told me with a trace of bitterness. "You've never been in love."

"I've got a brain, haven't I?"

"Sometimes I doubt it!" Trixie snapped. "Anyway, from the description of Eddie Price I got second hand from Thompson, Price isn't a large man. I insist the man who caught me by the throat was a little above average size."

"Maybe it was Colonel Humphries. Did you feel a beard?"

"No, and my hand was on his chin. I'm positive he had no beard."

"All of which is getting me dizzier and dopier," I confessed as I put the telegrams and letters in my pocket.

No telling what those letters contained. In a job like mine you can't be too squeamish. Especially when the case is big and as hot as this one was.

I was wondering how much Tommy Verne knew; how deeply he was involved, to cause that frantic state into which he had been jolted in his office—when someone rang the front door bell.

Trixie and I both jumped as the buzzer burred behind us. Trixie looked at me. I looked at her.

8

MYSTERY HOUSE

THE BUZZER WENT off again. Trixie started toward the light button.

"Leave it alone!" I warned in a whisper. "Whoever it is has seen the lighted windows. It'd just look worse if the light went out now."

And as the buzzer was pushed a third time I gestured toward the back of the room. "Behind those curtains! Out the back door if we have to! Here, take the flashlight and keep ahead of me! Wait, your purse?"

Trixie stepped quickly across the room and snatched her purse from the floor. We were almost to the drapes at the rear of the room when someone walked into the hall.

Beyond the drapes I turned and looked through a faint slit. It was like a stage—a small, faintly lighted stage, quiet and brooding with gruesome threat.

And onto that stage walked the jaunty figure of a tall, erect, broad-shouldered man. Jaunty—there was no other word for it. He carried a dark polished stick, wore spats and a well-tailored suit with a gay pattern of small checks, A soft hat was tilted slightly toward one eye.

He looked toward the back of the room. "Anybody

home?" he called in a mellifluous voice. On the silence that voice sounded startlingly incongruous.

No one answered. The late spring night was not cool, but he wore light mocha gloves turned down over the back of his hands. Slowly he removed the right glove and twisted the waxed ends of a small, gay, black mustache.

Appearance and assurance were those of a man with money and position. He seemed to know the house. He had entered without hesitation. He must be a friend of Dot Lancaster—and I couldn't figure what the devil he was doing here like this. Didn't he know she was out of town? Didn't he know she had a maid? An instant later he knew it. He looked toward the divan—and saw the dead woman.

He jumped back. Yes, jumped, and stood there stiff and staring. Then on his tiptoes, as if fearful he might be over-heard, he moved to the body and looked down at it. Then he fled. The last glimpse I got of his face on its way to the door showed an expression of utter bewilderment, consternation, and fear.

He didn't close the door; he simply vanished out of the room. It was plain he would keep on going until he was well down the street.

"The cops will be here next. He'll call them," I said.

Standing behind me, Trixie hadn't seen him. "Who was it?" she inquired hurriedly.

"I don't know. He saw the body and beat it. Let's go out the back way. Hold your breath and hope nothing happens."

Using my handkerchief again to kill fingerprints, I unlocked the back door. We stepped out into a small screened back porch; went down steps into a narrow back yard, walled on all sides. In the back wall was a gate, fastened by a spring lock. It opened easily enough from the inside. We stepped out into a narrow, paved alley, encountered no pedestrians or machines as we walked away.

HALF A MILE we walked through different streets, winding up on Riverside Drive. I waved down a taxi. Not until we were rolling through Columbus Circle and starting down Broadway did I draw a final breath of relief, for Trixie more than myself.

"That was a close shave," I said.

Trixie nodded.

"And all we got out of it, Mike, are a lot of questions which need answers."

"Maybe Thompson has got something out of that fellow. I'll call the office from Times Square."

I did. Thompson answered.

"Got anything to tell me?" I asked him.

"Plenty," Thompson gave me back fast. "Sir Douglas MacClain just telephoned to say his secretary, Price, is back in town."

"Ha! I thought so! How does he know?"

"Price returned to his rooming house late this afternoon. The landlady, scenting a possible reward, telephoned Sir Douglas."

"That old battleaxe would sell her grandfather down the river for the price of a can of stale coffee. What happened to Price?"

Thompson replied glumly. "The landlady apparently let Price know Sir Douglas and the police were looking for him. She reports Price hurried away rapidly with his suitcase."

"Trust her to wag that long tongue!" I groaned. "Listen, are you sure Price brought his suitcase to the house?"

"Sir Douglas said so."

"What about this Colonel Humphries?"

"He hasn't appeared in the picture as yet."

"Anything to report on Tommy Verne? Has that fellow I brought in talked?"

"Not a word. We're still checking the spots where Verne usually is found this time of the evening, but so far he hasn't been located."

"He won't be," I grunted.

"What's that? Do you know anything?" Thompson demanded.

"Plenty—but not enough. Have someone around your telephone all evening. I may call in at any moment."

"Wait! What's happened?" Thompson requested feverishly. But I hung up on him.

Without leaving the booth, I telephoned the Waldorf and asked if Colonel Humphries was registered.

"Colonel Jefferson Humphries registered this afternoon, but has checked out again," the clerk said.

"Checked in and *out* this afternoon?"

"Yes, sir."

Outside the booth Trixie took one look at me and spoke critically. "You look as if you've bitten into something sour, Mike."

"It could be worse. Eddie Price is back in town."

"Isn't he the little traveler!"

"Colonel Humphries is back too."

"I'm not surprised. They left together."

"The Colonel checked in at the Waldorf this afternoon—and checked right out again. Price went back to his old rooming house with his suitcase. The landlady leaked that he was wanted, and Price faded quick."

"And let the Colonel know—and the Colonel checked out quickly," Trixie guessed, looking pert and wise. "And where do we go from here, Mike?" says Trixie sweetly. "You're in charge, you know. Crowd that massive brain."

Scowling, I thought hard; abruptly said: "I've got one idea. It probably won't work, but it's worth a try. Let's shuttle over to Grand Central."

FROM THE GRAND Central I telephoned Thompson again. He was fit to tie. "What'd you hang up on me for?" he demanded.

"I was in a hurry. I still am. In exactly ten minutes I want you to throw that mug out and warn him away from Blaine operatives after this. Don't send anyone after him."

"Are you crazy? He'll get away."

"He might as well, for all the good he's doing you there. Toss him out. I know what I'm doing." And I hung up again before he could argue.

To Trixie I said: "Thompson's going to turn that fellow loose in ten minutes. He'll come out suspicious, looking for the catch. Of course he'll expect to be tailed. He's seen you once but the chances are he won't be looking for a woman. Follow him."

"Is that all, Mike, darling? And what will our hero be doing meanwhile?"

"I'll be tailing you. This fellow will get in contact with Tommy Verne or some of Verne's men right away. He'll want to tell them what happened to him."

We taxied away from the station toward the Madison

avenue building where the Blaine Agency offices were located; and Trixie said: "I didn't have a hat or coat on when he saw me. I've a pair of glasses here in my pocket-book I can use."

A moment later she had them on, looking so prim and severe that I hardly knew her. A deft touch or so like that and a subtle shift in personality could make Trixie hardly recognizable.

"One more thing," I went on. "If I lose you, get in touch with the office. I'll be in contact there also. Sure your gun's all right?"

"Quite. Are you looking for me to be caught also, Mike?"

I said, "Dry up!" and leaned forward and gave the driver instructions.

Ten minutes from the time I had called Thompson in the Grand Central, the setup was complete.

Across the street from the entrance to the building where our offices were located, Trixie was strolling. I was parked a quarter of a block back in the taxi with my eyes glued on her.

I didn't even see the fellow come out; but I did see Trixie begin to cover ground. She turned the next corner, toward the Grand Central. It was a one way street; my cab couldn't follow. I paid off the driver and hopped out. But by the time I got around the corner, Trixie was barely in sight ahead, making for the Grand Central.

By the time I got in the station Trixie was out of sight. On a hunch I went down to the shuttle. Maybe she'd gone that way, maybe not. A shuttle train was just pulling out for Times Square when I hit the top of the steps. So I took the following one over to Times Square, looked around for a few minutes and then called Thompson again.

"This is getting to be a habit," Thompson said nastily. "What happened to Verne's man?"

"Meehan's trailing him. She's to call you. I'll ring you back every five minutes. And in case you think this case is going to sleep, Dot Lancaster's maid was murdered this evening and Trixie Meehan almost got killed herself in the same room."

"Great snakes!" says Thompson. "Why didn't you tell me?"

"Later," says I. "And don't keep asking me what it's all about. I don't know. I'll call you back in five minutes!"

I smoked a cigarette and called Thompson back. He tried to question me and I hung up on him again. Four times I did that while Thompson rapidly became incoherent. The last time he said peevishly:

"She hasn't called yet!" But just as I started to hang up Thompson barked. "Wait a minute! The other telephone's ringing!"

Then he snapped back at me. "Miss Meehan is waiting for you at Thirty-sixth and Eighth Avenue!"

AND I WENT to that corner like a dog with a can on his tail, Trixie hailed me softly from a dark doorway.

"I almost lost him twice," Trixie said hurriedly. "He ducked through Times Square, took the subway to the Pennsylvania Station, and worked hard to shake off anyone who might be following him."

"Sure he didn't spot you?"

"I'm sure not. He went into one of those walk-ups in the next block. I've been watching the doorway. He's still inside."

"Great. You wait across the street from it and I'll go in. If I'm not out in five minutes, you'd better have it investigated."

"Absolutely not. I'm going in with you."

"One woman's been killed tonight. Stay out of this."

"I'm tough," said Trixie. "I'm going with you."

And she was. We went together.

Over there around Eighth Avenue you can find almost anything. We found lighted windows of a Greek grease joint. The steps creaked as we started up through odors of old cabbage and fried onions.

On the second floor, at the right, the blatting music of a radio, helped out by a crying baby, was sifting through a door. I knocked.

A fat house wife with her hair down in a skimpy braid opened the door and looked suspiciously at me. She was cradling the baby in one arm. Behind her two youngsters were playing on the floor.

"I'm looking for Mr. Rosenfeld, madam."

"I don't know no Rosenfeld." She turned, screeched back into the apartment. A masculine voice answered the music and she turned and shook her head again. "No—no Rosenfeld, mister."

A boy limped up behind her, holding a shoe in his hand.

"Maybe he means them men up on the third floor, ma. The ones that don't come in so much."

I said: "That sounds like it. Which apartment, buddy?"

"At the back on this side, mister."

We went up to the third floor. Up there the hall seemed smellier, the lights dimmer, the floor creakier.

"Pretend you're looking for a girl friend. If the door opens, get out of the way," I whispered.

No need to tell Trixie any more. She knew her lines on work like this. Her little heels tapped loudly back to the door in question.

"Harriet," she called to me in a shrill voice. "I wonder if this is where Jane lives. I'll knock and see."

Trixie banged gaily on the door and while she waited sang a few bars from a torch song in a more than audible voice.

Light glinted through the keyhole, but whoever was inside was in no hurry to open the door. Trixie knocked again. He must have slipped quietly to the door; a gruff voice suddenly asked:

"What is it?"

Trixie shrilled: "Does Jane Crosby live here?"

"No!" the voice replied irritably.

On our side of the door the situation was tense. If he didn't open up, what then?

Trixie juggled the uncertainty as skillfully as an old trouper doing an act. She giggled loudly.

"Of *course* it's not Jane's apartment. She's not married. Can you tell me which apartment she's in, mister? It's up here somewhere. Isn't it?"

"Never heard of her, lady. Try one of the other doors."

Trixie made a face at me, spoke pertly to him.

"Can't you open the door and give us some information? My feet are killing me."

Maybe it was that dopey crack about her feet. After a moment's pause a bolt inside rasped back. Trixie stepped back. The door opened—and I jumped in behind my gun.

9

INTO A TRAP

HE WASN'T LOOKING for it. I saw his hand start inside his coat; and I knocked half the wind out of him in a big, *"Oof!"* as I shoved my own gun in his belly. "Hold it!" I said. I meant it. He knew I meant it.

Shoulder high his hands went. Much harder, much meaner he was than the pudgy-faced man Trixie had followed. He had a broad angular jaw, corn-colored hair slightly mussed; his coat was off, his collar unbuttoned, as if he was all set to stay in for the evening. And he was boiling mad.

The Savage automatic, thirty-eight caliber, I found under his coat, didn't belong to a peaceful flat-dweller. So I warned him.

"If anyone else starts anything, you get it first!"

He thought I knew more than I did. He snarled: "That damned fool hasn't got a gun! Where's the rest of you?"

Trixie had moved in behind me. I said: "We're all here. Where's Con Craddock?"

He glared, said nothing as I pushed him back into the apartment. I was looking for a trap. The first thing I saw was Con Craddock, gagged and trussed in a chair so tightly he could hardly squirm.

Con made choked sounds behind the gag. I grinned at him. "Father is here," I said. "The nasty old ropes'll be off in a minute. Who else is in here?"

Con rolled his eyes, jerked his head toward a door at his left. I said to Trixie: "Put your gun in this man's back. Let him have it if he even coughs."

The door Con Craddock had indicated was not locked. A hinge squeaked as I opened the door. Fresh air swept out. Beyond a bed a window was up. The room was deserted.

"Lost him out the window," I thought, until I looked out that window and found a sheer drop of three stories. He would have needed wings to get out that way, and he hadn't had wings the last time I saw him. I looked further in the room.

Nothing under the bed. There was another door. When I opened it a high-pitched voice hastily exclaimed: "I haven't got no gun!"

He was uncommonly meek as he sidled out, eyeing my automatic, and dragged into the next room ahead of me. His partner swore at him.

"Shut up," I said. "Once a mug, always a mug. You fellows never learn. Untie Mr. Craddock."

The gag came off first. Con Craddock's face was red. He worked his mouth stiffly for a moment, then spoke thickly.

"I'll raise plenty of hell about this! Snatching a man right off the street this way! Those ropes were so tight I'll walk with a stoop for days! Mike, I understood they had you too."

"They did, but they couldn't keep me. What happened to you?"

"Nothing. I was brought here and tied up. Someone telephoned, heard I was here. That's all."

"No questions asked?"

"Not a one. Tommy Verne's behind this, of course. I'll drag him out in the open now, if it's the last thing I ever do!"

"It may be," I comforted him. "Verne's in deep now. There's been one murder this evening already."

Con stood up unsteadily, wincing as stiff muscles protested. "I thought I was going to be the first dead," he said. "Who was it?"

"Tell you later. Maybe these two know but I doubt it. This case is getting hot fast."

"I want Tommy Verne," Con Craddock growled. He caught the pudgy-faced one by the back of the neck. "Where is Verne?"

The fellow shrugged, shook his head.

Con hit him on the cheek. The fellow sat down hard, covered up with his arms and bleated: "I don't know anything about Verne! Honest t' God!"

"Hell!" said Con disgustedly. He turned to the bigger, meaner one. "You want some of it too?"

He got a sullen reply. "I don't know nothin' either. And don't make no passes at me!"

I'D ALWAYS THOUGHT of Con Craddock as being a soft-fingered columnist. But Con hit that big fellow on the nose, sank a left hook in his middle, and then slugged with both fists. The man tried to fight back but in less than three minutes Con gave him as sweet a shellacking as I've ever seen. At the finish the big fellow was backing off, trying to protect himself, insisting hoarsely:

"I don't know where Tommy Verne is. You'd better lay off! I've had enough!"

Con lifted an uppercut from his hip. It drove the fellow into the wall, and he went down groggily on the floor. Panting and rubbing his bruised knuckles, Con turned to me.

"I guess you're right. He doesn't know anything. Let's turn these two over to the police."

"Might as well," I agreed. "We'll need them both. But let me do the talking when the cops get here."

Con made the call, lighted a cigarette and grinned at Trixie. He was feeling better.

Heavy steps tramped outside the door. Two men from a radio patrol car crowded into the apartment. When they found Con Craddock had been kidnapped, the police force was at our disposal. The officer who handcuffed the big fellow took one look at the battered face and said: "You must have gone over this one with a steam roller, Mr. Craddock."

"I wish I had used a chair," Con said. "Take them down and book them on a kidnapping charge. My friend and I will appear against them."

We got down into the street with none of the occupants of the building being aware of what had happened.

"We'll grab a taxi and follow you," I said to the cops.

Agreeable as long as Con Craddock was involved, they drove off with their prisoners. We started toward the corner, watching for a taxi. As we walked I told Con what happened since I had last seen him. He was grave.

"It will make a swell newspaper story, won't it, Mike? It's getting pretty serious, isn't it?"

"Too blasted serious," I said. "I can't connive with murder. The police have got to know. I should have reported that woman's death. When we get to the station, I'll call up Thompson and tell him."

And just then Trixie caught my arm. "Mike! That auto that just passed! It had a platinum blonde in it!"

Con and I had the same thought. We turned. The machine which had just passed us was a big sedan. As we looked the tail lights blinked red, and it slowed to a stop in front of the building we had just left.

I ran back toward it, transferring my gun to a coat pocket.

A man got out, walked around to the sidewalk. He was the same size and build as Tommy Verne. I slowed to a walk; behind me Con did the same. It looked as if Verne was going to enter without seeing us. But something made him look our way. I don't know whether he recognized us or not; but he turned and ran back to his seat.

The rising snore of the speeding engine ripped out of the exhaust pipe at Con and me as we ran hard.

"Shoot at his tires!" Con panted.

BUT I DIDN'T do that as the automobile swung away from the curb and shot down the street. A taxi drew up with a squeal of brakes. Out its door Trixie called: "Here, Mike!"

Thinking quickly as usual, Trixie had done the one right thing at the right moment. I dove in it, snapping at the driver: "Follow that car!" Con followed, slamming the door. The taxi lurched ahead. Con panted: "Why didn't you shoot his tires?"

"There's a limit," I told him. "Taking shots around these streets is it." And to the driver I called: "Five dollars if you catch him!"

That helped some. He took us around the next corner after Tommy Verne as if we were heading straight down the street. Over here west of Broadway we had the streets almost to ourselves. But there was a limit to what that taxi motor could do. Verne knew the streets, knew how to drive. He doubled around corners like a gun-shy rabbit. His big, low slung car could turn faster, pick up speed quicker. The twin-tail lights drew farther ahead—and we lost them.

The driver slowed. "Want me to cruise around an' look for him?"

"Never mind," I said. "If you couldn't catch him while you could see him, you won't pick him up now. Drive up toward the park, and close that window."

He slipped the glass pane over and left us in privacy.

"That was Tommy Verne and Dot Lancaster," I said. "They were coming to call on you, Con. Figure that out."

Con growled: "I wish I'd been there!"

"It might not have been so nice. Verne is desperate."

"He ought to be now."

"He'll go to cover," I said. "It may be days before we can find him."

"Suits me; just so we get him."

"It doesn't suit me. I've got a case to crack. The police and newspapers will be digging into it in an hour or so. The Blaine Agency won't have any more chance of getting that half million in Liberty bonds than you'll have skating along the elevated if we let down now."

"All right," he said with resignation. "Go get your half million in Liberties. Where are they?"

"If I knew, I'd have them. But an idea has been rattling around for the last half hour. I'm going to call on Sir

Douglas MacClain and talk to him about it. We can place charges against those two later."

"Suits me," said Con, passing cigarettes. He was cheerful again. "I want an interview with MacClain anyway."

Sir Douglas had a house also. He lived on East Sixty-third Street, and the place must have set him back plenty.

A manservant answered my ring. "Is MacClain in?" I asked.

"If you are referring to Sir Douglas MacClain, sir, whom shall I say is calling?"

"Harris—from the Agency."

"Beg pardon, sir?" he said with his nose in the air.

"From the Agency. Tell him that. He'll understand."

He closed the door and left us standing there. "When I get my second million," I said, "I'm going to hire a man like that and make him stand eight hours a day in front of a mirror making faces at himself."

Trixie said, "When you make your second million! If you weren't so lowbrow, you'd take him as a matter of course."

A moment later the door opened again and we were informed: "Sir Douglas MacClain will see you in the drawing room. This way please."

We followed him down a hallway.

Sir Douglas was standing in a large drawing room as we walked in. He looked as starchy and crotchety as ever. But his red face seemed a trifle paler. It may have been the lighting.

"Er—good evening, Harris," he greeted me.

I almost pinched myself. The stiff bow, the cold nasty manner were strangely absent. The man appeared almost glad to see me. He didn't even glare at Con and Trixie. To make it even more amazing he added:

"I wasn't expecting you this evening." Over the welcome, which was almost furtive, lay a curious restraint of movement.

"I didn't know I was coming," I said. "This is Miss Meehan, who is working with me, and Mr. Con Craddock, who writes a daily column on Broadway, which you've undoubtedly read." Then I set myself for the explosion about Con.

NONE CAME. SIR Douglas bowed stiffly to Trixie and Con Craddock. "How do you do?" he said. "Won't you—er—sit down?"

We did. Sir Douglas remained standing, facing us. He said nothing. We said nothing. Queer how that room dropped into quiet; almost ominous quiet. Without knowing why, I suddenly had the feeling that we had walked into danger again.

Trixie sensed it. She was sitting forward in her chair, fumbling with the catch of her purse, where she could get to her little automatic if necessary.

I broke the awkward silence.

"I came here to ask you a few questions about Price and this Colonel Humphries, Sir Douglas."

Beneath the stiff, straw-colored mustache, his mouth opened soundlessly. In amazement, or fear? "Er—uh—Price?"

"Yes."

"My dear fellow, I don't know that I—ah—care to talk about that just now. This is hardly the time or place."

I did pinch myself then. Actually. This couldn't be the

man I had talked to in Thompson's office. He looked the same and had the same timbre of voice, but something was wrong, decidedly wrong. After all the hell he had raised about Colonel Humphries and Price, why didn't he want to talk about them now? Not because of Trixie and Con Craddock. The Sir Douglas whom I had met at the Blaine Agency would have had no hesitation in saying so. I began to get mad.

"It's the time and place," I said. "Plenty has happened. I want to get some answers from you."

"Please, young man. Some other time," Sir Douglas begged, approaching my chair.

Standing, I let him have it cold turkey. "You want your Liberty bonds, don't you?"

"Er—ah—"

He continued to ease on around me and suddenly I saw that, although he was facing me, his eyes were sliding furtively toward heavy window drapes at the side of the room.

"What's over there?" I snapped at him.

He went crazy. I thought so anyway. A jump put him behind my chair, with me between him and the window drapes.

"They're behind those curtains!" he cried excitedly. "Shoot before he kills you!"

10

THE MISSING LIBERTIES

WHAT WOULD YOU do? So did I. Two seconds later, as my automatic came out with my thumb sliding the safety off, I was six feet away from that chair. Trixie was on her feet with her hand coming out of her purse.

But no shots greeted us.

"Who's going to kill me?" I snapped at Sir Douglas.

"Humphries! He's behind the curtains. Price is with him!"

That put new light on the matter. I said: "I'm dizzy, but I'll put a couple of shots through the curtains for luck."

From behind the curtains a sonorous voice called hastily: "That would be murder, not luck! We're coming out, hands in the air, and not a gun between us. Out with you, Eddie. I've done the best I can for you."

They emerged from the recess behind the curtains and I stared speechlessly.

Price I knew at a look. Medium height, slender, a bit stoop-shouldered, his blue suit did not fit so well, and his small blond mustache shaded a weak mouth. His face was pale and his hands were trembling.

The other man was taller and bulwarked with assurance. His gray felt hat, which he had continued to wear in the house, was tilted at a jaunty angle. His well-tailored suit had a gay pattern of small checks; he wore spats and carried a dark polished stick. The waxed points of his small black mustache jerked up as he smiled affably at us.

"Put up your artillery," he said to us jovially. "MacClain is having nightmares. A pen-knife is the most dangerous weapon we have."

From behind my chair Sir Douglas warned: "That stick he's carrying is a weapon! It can shoot!"

"It won't," I promised him. "Drop it, you! And who the devil are you?"

This affable, smiling person with the black stick and perfect self-possession was the man who had entered Dot Lancaster's house, taken one look at the dead woman and fled.

He dropped his stick on the rug and addressed me airily, "Are you satisfied, young man?"

"I haven't started to be. Humphries, eh? Just a minute." I stepped to him and reached for his hat.

He moved back smiling. "Quite right, young man. I'm wearing a black wig, and my beard has been removed and my mustache is dyed. I'll be glad to answer any other questions which may be disturbing you."

"They threatened me!" Sir Douglas MacClain said hoarsely. "Refused to let me do more than dismiss my servant. When Edwards answered your ring, Humphries ordered me to send him on back to his quarters after admitting you, while he and Price stood behind these drapes and listened to what was being said. Humphries warned me he would shoot with that dashed stick at the slightest provocation. I stood there talking to you, not knowing at what moment a bullet would be put in my back."

Humphries chuckled and pushed his stick toward me with a foot. "Have a look at it, young man," he suggested. "It was quite harmless, MacClain."

"Sir Douglas MacClain, you bloody bounder!"

Colonel Humphries dropped his aplomb. His face grew hard. "Don't start calling names," he warned curtly.

And I said: "That goes for both of you. Humphries, what's the idea of shedding your beard and glasses and changing your appearance this way?"

Under his waxed mustache white teeth flashed at me. "I have peculiar habits, young man."

"You picked a funny time to exercise them."

He dismissed that with a wave of his hand. "One person's opinion is as good as another's. I chose to do so. My privilege, eh?"

PRICE WAS STANDING there biting his lower lip, looking very unhappy. "Where have you been?" I asked him.

"Uh—Buffalo."

"Why did you come back?"

"Why—why—"

"Don't answer him, Eddie," Humphries advised in a fatherly manner. "You don't have to talk."

Sir Douglas was back in form again, "Arrest them!" he directed me loudly and nastily.

"I thought you didn't want an arrest."

"I've changed my mind! After this visit, I see I shan't be safe, and there is the matter of the bonds to be settled. The police had better do it now, I suppose."

Humphries twisted an end of his mustache. His eyes,

studying me, were dark, keen. But beneath his jauntiness I saw that he was uneasy. Trixie was standing watchfully, gun in hand. Con Craddock was taking it in with absorbed interest.

Humphries slowly lifted his eyebrows. "I'd be interested to know what bonds the police can do anything about. Personally I never deal in bonds."

"Someone dealt in these," I told him. "We're looking for half a million in Liberty bonds that disappeared out of the office safe when Price went to Buffalo."

His hand stayed at the tip of his mustache for a moment. His glance moved to Price inquiringly. "Hear that, Eddie? Half a million in bonds?"

Price licked his lips. "I don't know anything about them," he denied huskily.

"You're not lying to me, Eddie?"

"Of course not!"

"Stop this farce!" Sir Douglas roared indignantly. "The bonds are gone! It's plain who got them! Let the police get the truth out of them!"

"I'd like a little of that truth first," I decided. "Humphries, what were you doing with that dead woman in Miss Lancaster's house this evening?"

The question staggered Humphries. The jaunty air vanished. Standing there staring at me, Humphries aged in seconds. He opened his mouth to say something, then closed it without speaking.

Sir Douglas uttered two horrified words. *"Dead woman?"*

And curtly I said: "Very dead. Who killed her? Someone's going to the electric chair for it."

Price uttered a moan and charged blindly toward the back of the room.

"*Trixie, don't shoot!*" I yelled.

I could have shot Price, but I didn't. Con Craddock was nearest the back of the room. When I saw Con launch himself across the rug I stood there and watched. He caught Price. They careened off a chair. Price sobbed:

"I won't go to the electric chair! I won't! I've had enough! Let me out of here or I'll kill you!"

But he wasn't killing anyone this night. Con shoved him off to arm's length and hit him in the jaw. Price's knees buckled; Con had to hold him off the floor. Dragging him back, Con dumped him in a chair.

"I guess you know who killed her now," Con said breathing heavily.

"It looks like Price, doesn't it?" I agreed. "Eh, Humphries?"

"That," he said "is open to proof."

"Why did you and Price go to Buffalo?"

He smiled. "Would you believe it, my suspicious young friend, I went to give a bride away. Nothing else."

"Did you?"

"Unfortunately no. The bride did not appear, so we returned."

"Why didn't she appear?"

"Who knows the workings of a woman's mind?" Colonel Humphries sighed. "Love is a delicate passion, easily swayed."

"You'll be quoting poetry next. Who was the intended bride?"

I had him there. If he answered truthfully, he would be

connected to the dead woman through Dot Lancaster. He carried it off smoothly.

"Since she backed out, we'll protect her. Eh, Eddie? Not a word about her."

Eddie nodded dumbly. He was slumped in the chair where Con Craddock had dropped him.

"I'll speak of it," I said. "It was Dot Lancaster."

Sir Douglas MacClain snorted. "You seem to know quite a bit, Harris. However, I insist you call the police."

"I'm not ready."

"Damme!" he blazed in sudden passion. "Are you giving me orders? Consider your agency discharged from this case! The police will recover my bonds!"

"Right now," I said, "we're trying to find who committed a murder in Miss Lancaster's apartment. In case you're interested, I know who did it."

His face was red and furious. "We know who did it! The police will have a signed statement out of Price!"

"I doubt it—because Price didn't do it."

"What's that? If Price didn't, who did? Humphries?"

Colonel Humphries' face grew interested as he looked at me. I had the feeling he was looking past me at something. Before I could turn a voice at my shoulder purred:

"We'll find out who killed her. The cops can have their turn later."

11

ROBBERY BY PROXY

A HAND REACHED past my shoulder for my automatic. A gun at my back carried more threat than the purring voice. Tommy Verne's voice went on:

"Get the woman's gun. Frisk the rest of them. Come in, Dot."

Verne had brought two men with him. They looked worse than the couple Con and I had turned over to the police. Their suits weren't even pressed. It was a safe bet they hadn't been eating too steadily lately.

Trixie surrendered her gun without argument. Verne's two men frisked everybody, stepped back, stood watchfully, hands ready in their coat pockets.

Dot Lancaster had walked in silently and sat down in the chair nearest Trixie Meehan. La Lancaster was prettier than her picture. She was a knockout. To think of her falling for a shoddy piece like Eddie Price was laughable.

Colonel Humphries regarded her with a stunned look. "Eddie, is this the young woman you were to marry?" he questioned.

Eddie nodded, licked his lips, spoke to her huskily. "We—we waited for you in Buffalo, Dot. I telegraphed you twice, and then we came back. What—what was the matter?"

She ignored him. For all her looks, Dot Lancaster looked as if she had been drawn through a half-sized keyhole. Her face was pale; back of her make-up was the same inner tired look I had noticed on Tommy Verne's face.

One of Verne's men had slipped out of the room. He came back now with the manservant, who was agitated, upset.

"Is—is this a robber, Sir Douglas?" the man stammered.

"Talk when I tell you to!" Verne snapped at him. "Let's get down to business. Craddock, I wasn't looking for you and your friend here."

Con answered grimly. "We're here, Tommy. And all the muscle men you can rake up won't get you out of this. Those two mugs you turned loose on Harris and me are already under arrest."

"I figured that. I've sent my lawyer to bail them out."

Verne had stepped back away from me. Turning, I saw him pass a hand over his forehead as if he were weary or in pain, but when the hand dropped, the thin sallow face was hard, threatening.

"Who is this friend of yours?" Verne asked Craddock. He indicated me.

"I'm working for the Blaine International Agency."

"I thought you must be a dick. What do you think you know? Who killed Dot's maid?"

"Not so fast," I said. "I'll tell you a few facts first. Sir Douglas MacClain here has custody of a two million dollar trust fund. This week he went to Montreal. While he was gone, half a million dollars of that trust fund, in Liberty bonds, was taken from the safe. No one else had the combination. Price was the secretary. He could have gotten the combination. He vanished at the same time the bonds did. Humphries there went with him. When Sir Douglas returned and discovered the loss, he put the Blaine Agency on the case. Price claims he went to Buffalo to marry Miss Lancaster. Humphries says he went along to give the bride away. I'd like to know why he went clear up to Buffalo on an errand like that."

Humphries smiled reminiscently. "In discussing the possible sale of a block of shares to MacClain, I spent enough time around the office to become acquainted with Price. He confided that he was in love and was going to elope to Buffalo. Since MacClain was running up to Montreal for some days, I decided to kill time by going to Buffalo and seeing Price married."

"That the only reason?"

COLONEL HUMPHRIES SMILED deprecatingly.

"It is barely possible I might have collected dividends on the effort," he admitted. "A friend in MacClain's office would have done me no harm. When the bride failed to appear, Price and I returned."

"And Price tipped you off the police wanted you both, so you checked out again in a hurry."

"Why deny it?" Humphries admitted gracefully. "I also dispensed with my beard, dyed my mustache and changed my personality somewhat, so that I might have leisure to find out why I was wanted by the police. Price didn't seem to know."

"You got Miss Lancaster's address from Price and went to see her."

We were back at the dead woman again. Humphries stopped smiling.

"I'm not admitting that, young man, but, had I done so, it would have been logical to ask the young lady what she knew of the peculiar state of affairs."

"Logical, also, I suppose, after you found the body in Miss Lancaster's house, to come here to see MacClain?"

"Had I found a body, yes."

"You're not sure whether Price killed the woman or not?"

"I am only an acquaintance of Price, young man."

Tommy Verne moved close to me again, speaking harshly. "I'm sick of all this. Who killed Dot's maid?" I was watching MacClain.

"Take a look at him, Trixie," I said, "massaging the finger off which he's pried a ring this evening. He did it and my guess is he stole the bonds. How about it, MacClain?"

Trixie cried: "Good boy, Mike! I was wondering if you'd see it. I've been watching the back of his other hand, where I scratched it! He's the one who tried to kill me at Miss Lancaster's apartment!"

Tommy Verne burst out laughing. Wild, uncontrollable, hard laughter, it was not quite sane.

"Dot! Do you hear that? Do you get it? MacClain did it!"

And she cried, "Tommy, darling!" And jumped up and hugged him.

Sir Douglas MacClain blasted at me with wild, furious indignation.

"You're utterly mad! You fool! Do you realize what you're saying? You're accusing me of murder; accusing me of stealing my own bonds!"

I faced his manservant. "Sir Douglas has been wearing a ring on his left hand, hasn't he?"

"Why—ah—"

"Don't lie to me! I saw it today! What happened to it?"

"Why, sir, I really don't know, sir. Isn't the ring there?"

"Shut up, you fool!" Sir Douglas raged at him. "Don't you see he's trying to damage me with your testimony?"

"Is there a wall safe in the house?" I snapped at the manservant.

"Why—why—"

"Dammit!" I said, grabbing him by the arm. "Do you want to be charged with aiding and abetting murder?"

"Oh, no, sir; no, indeed, sir! Nothing of the kind, sir! I have the best references! There is a wall safe, I believe, sir! Upstairs in the master's bedroom. Behind a picture."

"Now if we can get in that safe," I said, turning away from him.

"Try it, Dabney," Verne said to one of his men. "I've heard you used to be pretty good at that."

The man grinned sheepishly and started out of the room.

"We'll all go up," I said. "I want to see what comes out of that safe."

"Fair enough," Tommy Verne declared.

We crowded the large bedroom. While Dabney went to work on the wall safe, Trixie delved in the drawers of a big dresser.

"Here it is, Mike!" she cried suddenly. Turning, she held up a massive gold ring set with a large stone seal. "I can almost feel it pressing in my neck again!" Trixie said, making a face at the memory.

Dabney gave a grunt of satisfaction. The safe door swung open. He reached in and brought out a bundle of bonds.

THE CRASHING REPORT of a revolver behind us took everyone by surprise.

Dot Lancaster screamed.

Sir Douglas MacClain had fallen back on the bed. The revolver in his hand lay across the disarranged pillow, from under which he must have secured it.

Tommy Verne drew a deep breath. "He had it coming to him," he said, hard and bitter. "But I wish he'd had guts enough to keep going and get some of the hell he's put me through the last few months."

"He acted like he'd never seen you before, Verne."

Tommy Verne lighted a cigarette. His hands were trembling. For that matter we were all shaky.

"MacClain didn't know me," Verne said. "In London several years ago he gave Dot a rush. You might as well know. We're tired of dodging it. Dot got into some trouble in England over the theft of a diamond bracelet. It was circumstantial evidence, but damaging. She managed to get back here to New York, changed her name, bleached her hair out and got a job dancing in one of my night clubs.

"We fell for each other hard and were going to get married when MacClain showed up at Dot's house one evening. He'd recognized her and followed her home. He reminded her that Scotland Yard was looking for her, and suggested she be nice to him. Dot wouldn't have any of that, of course. But MacClain made her promise to see him often. Dot came straight to me with it."

Tommy Verne clenched a fist unconsciously; his voice shook as he went on.

"I blew up. Dot couldn't let me have him knocked off. She said we were both going straight now. MacClain had a real title. His death or disappearance would mean an investigation. Dot might be dragged into it, so I laid off.

"I even quit seeing Dot publicly," said Tommy Verne. "MacClain didn't know about me. She was afraid if he did know, he might tip off Scotland Yard. She kept stringing him along, trying to find a way out.

"Then, not long ago, he said he had a little job for her. His secretary, Price, had been stealing money to spend on a girl, MacClain claimed, but he couldn't prove it. He wanted to trap Price. Dot was to make Price fall for her on the theory that he'd need more money and would steal more recklessly. MacClain promised to forget what he knew about her if she did it. Dot agreed. Price fell for her all right—but he got marriage on the brain. Dot told MacClain the thing had gone far enough. Price was threatening at suicide if they weren't married.

"MacClain told her to kid him along; to even make a date to be married. He suggested that she agree to elope to Buffalo. Dot refused. MacClain told her to at least promise to meet Price out of town. He'd steal the money to go there. She wouldn't have to go. It went through on that basis.

"Dot went down to Baltimore to see an aunt, and then on to Washington yesterday, and came back here this evening. Meanwhile," said Tommy Verne, "Craddock showed up in my office and got to prying into Dot's past. I was half crazy with worry, not knowing how everything would turn out. I didn't know what was happening, but I could see something was wrong. All I could think of was trying to protect Dot. I followed you two out of the office myself, saw you go into Danny's and got a couple of men I knew to pick you both up when you came out. I just wanted to hold you until Dot got off the train this evening and I could talk it over with her."

He sounded apologetic, and I nodded. He continued:

"But Dot didn't know anything more than I've just told you. We started up to face Craddock with it but when I got out of the car and saw you two on the sidewalk, I knew there'd been another slip.

"So I got a couple more men," said Tommy Verne grimly, "and came here to have it out with MacClain."

HIS VOICE WAS shaking when he finished. His arm was around Dot Lancaster. Looking at them I had some faint idea of what they must have gone through.

"MacClain settled it," I said. "It's plain enough what he was doing. He had a respectable name, a two million dollar trust fund in his care—and no money of his own. He wanted to get his hands on some of that trust money. To do it with any chance of success he had to pin it cold on someone else. Price was the punk. The idea was almost fool proof. Price leaving town at the same time the bonds vanished, and later unable to produce the girl he was supposed to have met, would smash his alibi. MacClain alibied himself by going straight to the Blaine Agency and placing the case in our hands. He gave *carte blanche* to make any moves necessary to get the money back. His story was reasonable, his request for secrecy not illogical. He knew there would be publicity because the money would not be found. But the testimony of the Blaine Agency would automatically shift suspicion away from him."

Dot Lancaster spoke to me in a small voice. "Did he really kill my maid? I haven't been home yet."

"He did," I said. "And by the way, here are some letters of yours. You were merely lucky. MacClain had the bonds and every chance of getting away with them. But after the publicity, what? You were dangerous. He had to shut your mouth. He either got your maid in the dark by mistake, thinking she was you, or he found out from her that you were due back this evening—and cleared the way to wait for you.

"Miss Meehan and I went to your house. In the dark MacClain caught her by the throat and tried to kill her too. He was wearing the seal ring. It dug into her throat so hard she remembered it. And she scratched the back of his hand. I ran in and frightened him off. He evidently had intelligence enough to know the ring might be damaging evidence. As soon as he got home he removed it; must have been quite a job getting it off and hurt his finger. He couldn't keep from massaging the spot while he was talking to us. The red band where the ring had been was visible. He had no way of knowing that Miss Meehan was the one he had choked, or I was the one who had frightened him off. He should have been more careful with his hands. The minute I spotted that finger, I knew the rest."

Colonel Humphries had been staring at the bed. Now he cocked his hat at a jauntier angle, twirled one waxed point of his mustache. "To think," he murmured, "that I picked MacClain for a dumb Britisher who might be interested in some excellently engraved gold mining shares. And all the time he was making a sucker out of me. Well—live and learn. What do we do now?"

"Call the police and turn the mess over to them," I said. "Including these bonds. And as far as I'm concerned, I never heard that Miss Lancaster was ever in England. Anybody here feel different? How about you, Price?"

"I never was in England," said Eddie Price.

"Then we'll all live and let live. Let's go downstairs and wait for the cops."

Trixie joined me as we left the room. "Live and learn," she sniffed. "You may live, but you'll never learn, Mike."

"Now what?"

"If I had talked to Mr. Verne two minutes about his girl, I could have told you he was in love with her, and they were both probably straight."

"I talked ten and didn't know it."

"Ape! Sometimes I marvel that you ever get by," said Trixie scornfully.

And so we came to the end of another case fighting.

NITRO! NITRO!

*An Oil Field on a Boom—Men Mad
with the Lust for Liquid Gold—and a
Diabolic Phantom Killer in Their Midst*

1

OIL FIELD MURDER

THERE HE LAY like a stuck pig. The shock of it stunned me mute, motionless. Yes, me, Mike Harris, of the Blaine Agency. Sure, this Jack Davidson wasn't a pig; he hadn't squealed. He hadn't made a sound. But it was as messy.

He lay in the back room of that Sandy Pool oil field office, not yet twenty-five, broad-shouldered, good-looking in his laced boots, khaki suit and flannel shirt. One moist black curl was down over his tanned forehead in the careless way a boy's mother would love to pat back into place. Any mother would have been proud of the man Jack Davidson had become. And he lay there with the ghost of a peaceful grin on his face and a bone-handled knife buried in his throat.

Just beyond him a drawn window shade slatted softly in the evening breeze. Above his feet a big calendar picturing a half-nude dancing girl rippled lazily on the plank wall.

A cold chill crawled up my spine. Yes, my spine. Me, Mike Harris. For that whispering draft of wind rumpled Jack Davidson's hair as if death lingered, caressing him. And the sloe-eyed wench on the rippling calendar seemed to be doing a slow, macabre dance as she smiled down at his body.

*Thompson was saying, "That's
the best way, Simpson. Take
'em both in your truck"*

A whispering breeze on a dead man's black curls—a lithographed nude doing a smiling dance of death over a corpse. Phew! Cold sweat sprang out on my forehead.

Don't laugh. Ten minutes before I'd have laughed too. But here it was in the crystal clarity of a sudden nightmare. High overhead in the night sky the plane that had dropped me at the crude little landing field beyond the derricks droned eastward again.

The smiling pilot had told me he'd be back in Kansas City before ten this evening. But I wouldn't be. I'd be here in Sandy Pool, this roaring little boom oil town near the Texas-Oklahoma border, with a murder mystery on my hands, and death skulking in the night outside.

The clerk in the outer office stopped typing and said, "Isn't he there?" His voice sounded hollow, queer against the silence.

I laughed, without turning my head.

"Yes, he's here," I said.

I heard his chair scrape back, heard his steps come toward me. Three words were all I'd said, but they brought him to the doorway behind me, looking over my head.

He said, "Wh-what's happened?"

"What d'you think's happened?" I snapped, glad of the chance to work off a few jittery nerves. "Do you think he's doing a dress rehearsal?"

I moved aside for the clerk to enter the room. But he hung back in the doorway, eyes popping, weak chin slack.

"My God!" he gulped. "Who did it? Where's the man who did it? Is he in here? Oh, Lord! What will his father say?"

So I reached up and slapped his sallow cheek.

"Stop that!" I snarled. "If you can't look like a man, try to act like one! You told me to go right on in. Why didn't you get up and tell him I was here?"

THAT STOPPED HIS hysteria. But his thin-lipped mouth

was opening, closing like the mouth of a stranded fish. He looked sick, frightened, as he gangled there in the doorway, a head taller than me.

I hadn't liked him at first sight. Now I liked him less. Tall, bony, sharp-faced, stooped, his hair and eyebrows were a bleached yellow. His nose was small and sharp, and his thin-lipped mouth was mean, tight above the weak chin.

His stuttered answer was half a groan.

"Mr. Davidson was checking some d-drilling reports. There wasn't any use in t-telling him you were here. He was expecting you. You d-don't think *I* know anything about it, do you?"

"I don't think anything," I gave him. "Wasn't there any noise in this back room?"

He shook his head, passed a handkerchief over his face with a shaking hand.

"The typewriter was making a lot of noise. I didn't hear a thing. As long as Mr. Davidson d-didn't call, I had no reason to th-think anything was wrong."

"And he was in here alone?"

"Y-yes."

"Stop stuttering!" I snapped. "Do you know who I am?"

"No," he denied.

"Do you know why I'm here?"

"No," he groaned, passing the soiled handkerchief over his sallow face again. "Who are you? What was your business with Mr. Davidson?"

That question was going to have to be answered. Jack Davidson wasn't here to help me now. From him I'd never get the details of the case that had brought me here. His murder was evidently only another angle of the matter. So I lied cheerfully.

"My name's Harris. I'm here for some reports on the Davidson leases. When was the last time you saw Davidson alive?"

He looked at his watch. "About thirty-five minutes ago. He came in for a drink of water."

"And you've been typing ever since?"

He gulped, nodded.

The wind was still whispering past the window curtain. I stepped over the body, lifted the curtain and looked out the open window.

The night was moonless, dark. Beyond the window a vacant lot was cluttered with odds and ends of dismantled oil derricks and drilling supplies. Beyond that, beyond the dim side street in front of the little building, were the shacks, the tents, the roistering twenty-four-hour life of this new oil town.

This was the fourth boom town I'd worked in for the Blaine Agency. They are all alike; some a little better, some a little worse.

A wildcatter, or one of the companies proves up a pool with a discovery well, and the lid comes off. Assorted hell flies to the spot, like iron filings to a magnet. Legitimate and illegitimate, good and bad they come—drilling crews, truckers, teamsters, merchants, sharpers, wives (not so many of them), and the oil town girls looking for easy money. Rich man, poor man, beggar man, thief—all tossed together in the mad, wild scramble for quick money, easy money, and the devil take the hindmost.

And here was young Jack Davidson, who had brought

in the discovery well on a lease owned by his father's Big Sandy Oil Company, dead, with a knife in his throat.

OUT THERE IN the night were a thousand men and plenty of women, who might have slipped through this open window, stabbed him, climbed out and vanished in the darkness with no one the wiser.

By the size and style of the knife it was hard to believe a woman had driven it to the hilt in his tanned throat. Most women would use a small knife, on the dagger or stiletto style. Not this man-sized hunting knife.

On the other hand, there would be women out there capable of swinging a machete, if it were handy.

"What's your name?" I threw at the clerk.

"Gillis," he said.

So I let him have it nastily. "Who do you think did this?"

"I don't know," Gillis groaned.

"Who's made threats against him?" He blinked. "Threats?"

"You heard me."

He blinked, looked uneasy. "Why—why—"

Just then the front door opened with a bang. A bull-base voice bellowed: "Where's Jack Davidson? Where's those extra men and guns I was to get? How can I get my drilling done with hell on my heels all the time? Another man slugged half an hour ago, by Godfrey, and the rest of my roughnecks wild over it! Let's get this thing settled right now!"

So I says, "You won't settle anything by shouting. Jack Davidson's dead."

2

PETE YOUNGER

HE WOULD HAVE made two of Gillis, the clerk, and three of me. He was the toughest-looking customer I've ever seen. Take six feet and add seven inches on it. Hang on a pair of shoulders half as broad, fasten on ape-like arms with hands like meat crushers. Put it in overalls tucked inside leather boots smeared with mud and crude black oil, an overall jacket with a rip on one shoulder and a weather-beaten sombrero cocked over one eye. Put an uncut black beard on a face marked by a big, bold nose and glaring eyes under shaggy, black brows—and you have him.

He stopped beyond the door and glared down at me. "Somebody else dead, huh?" he demanded; loudly; "Who is it? Who in hell are you? Gillis, damn your pussy-footing soul, where's Jack Davidson?"

Gillis gulped. "He just told you, Mr. Younger."

"Have a look," I invited.

So he looked. He ducked on through the doorway, went to the body and stared down in silence for a moment. Then a huge hand grabbed the sombrero off his head and he began to curse in a low, terrible rumble which seemed to shake the room.

I've heard men swear. I've seen strong men in wild fury.

But what I saw and heard in the next few moments left me dumb and gaping. That big stranger cursed in three languages with a fluency I'd have thought impossible. There, over that body, he promised that hell would seem a paradise to the man who had killed Jack Davidson.

But through it all was a vein of raw grief, which told plainer than tears the affection he had had for Jack Davidson.

When he ran down for a moment, I said, "You can't do anything about it by swearing. Got any idea who did it?"

He swung on me, clapping his big hat on his head. A big thumb indicated me as he spoke to Gillis.

"Who's this little red-haired shrimp?"

I never worry about being called a shrimp. I am a shrimp, so what of it? The bigger they are the harder they fall. Two hundred pounds of meat too often has a peanut for a brain. So I grinned faintly when Gillis rolled his eyes at me and said:

"His name's Harris. He just arrived on that plane to see Mr. Davidson."

Still to Gillis, the big fellow said, "What about?"

"Our leases," he said.

"A lease-hound, hey?" the giant rumbled, glowering at me. "Who you with, Harris?"

"Maybe," I cracked, "you'd better telephone his father in Kansas City. The old man will have to know about this anyway. Before you hang up, let me have a little bit of a talk with him."

A battered desk in the corner held a telephone. He glowered at me for another moment—I had the feeling he'd have glowered at anyone just then—and then put through a call to Jack Davidson, Sr., in Kansas City. And when he spoke to that urbane oil multimillionaire; I got another surprise. This wild giant's voice went husky and shaking as he said:

"Jack, this is Pete Younger. I'd rather cut off my arm than tell you this, Jack. It's—it's hell!… No, the wells are all right. It's the boy, Jack. He's here in the back office. Somebody put a knife in his throat… Yeah, Jack—dead."

If grief ever hits me suddenly, I hope somewhere in the world there's a friend to reach out over hundreds of miles as that big fellow did before my eyes, and say as he did, huskily. "Jack, my arm's around your shoulder and I'm here, like always. What you want I should do? There's a little redheaded fellow here named Harris who says you know about him."

No, no tears. Big Jack Davidson, in Kansas City, didn't go to pieces. He wasn't that kind of a man. I could hear his voice; rasping steadily in the receiver. It stopped. Pete Younger thrust the telephone at me.

"Here," he said, and he wasn't glowering now.

IN KANSAS CITY, seven hours earlier, I had lunched with Big Jack Davidson. Over the wire now his voice sounded very little different.

"I'm glad you're there, Harris. Will you do what you can in this matter? Pete Younger will help you. He's my drilling superintendent, and my oldest and closest friend. I've told him about you. I'm leaving for there at once."

That was all. The two men were staring at me when I turned away from the telephone. Pete Younger spoke gruffly, but without animosity.

"Gillis says you found him."

"I did," I said. "And I'm wondering who he knew well enough to let through that open window when it would have been easier to come through the front door."

Gillis pressed his lips together and remained silent.

Pete Younger ran thick fingers through his ragged black beard, and looked at me helplessly. In physical action he was formidable. The tangled leads of this mystery made him uncertain.

"It does look funny, don't it?" he said.

And I said, "Davidson knew there was a reason for the person to come in through the window. Whatever talking they did was in low voices, close together."

Gillis cleared his throat. "How do you know they talked?"

"Nobody would have come through that window and stepped close enough to Davidson to stab him, without saying something. They weren't fighting. They weren't even arguing, or their voices would have risen loud enough for you to hear. The visit was friendly enough, even if it was secretive, and before Davidson suspected anything, he had a knife in his throat. Funny you didn't hear him hit the floor."

Gillis batted his eyes at me. "My typewriter makes a lot of noise when I'm working fast."

"What were you about to tell me when Mr. Younger came in? Something about someone threatening him?" I tossed at him.

Gillis moistened his thin lips, flicked a glance at Younger, looked at me.

"I wasn't going to say anything. You didn't hear me right," he denied.

Pete Younger moved quicker than I thought a man of

his size could move. His ham-like hand slapped down on the clerk's long, thin neck. His voice rumbled ominously:

"Holding out, are you, Gillis? I never cared much for you—and if you're covering up something now, God help you!"

He didn't choke the clerk. But Gillis's bony shoulders seemed to cringe under the weight of the big hand.

"You haven't any right to talk to me like that, Mr. Younger," he protested indignantly. "Let go of my neck. I—I won't be bullied!"

"No?" Younger growled.

With one hand, as easily and carelessly as if he had been moving a feather duster, he shook Gillis until the man's face was purple, he was gulping for breath and his pale blue eyes were bulging.

"I'll—I'll t-tell you e-even if I am w-wrong." Gillis stammered; and when Younger stopped shaking him, Gillis panted, "Cass Cameron was in here this afternoon talking to Mr. Davidson. They were both mad. I heard Cameron say, 'I'll show you you can't get away with it! You'll get the surprise of your life, damn you!'"

Younger removed his hand. "Cass Cameron," he growled thoughtfully. "What were they talking about?"

"I don't know," Gillis denied nervously.

"What else did they say?"

"That's all I heard."

Younger turned on his heel, stared at the body, and then gave me a helpless glance.

"We'll have to do something about him," he said. "I'll notify Joe Moss, the deputy sheriff, so he can't complain. I guess old man Harker, the sheriff, will come charging over and make a fuss."

Younger tramped out.

Gillis was scowling after him when I said, "Got a flashlight handy?"

He took one from a desk drawer. I went outside and examined the ground under the open window. The hard-baked earth held no shoe marks. No bloody prints were on the windowsill. For that matter, none had been on the knife handle.

Somehow I had the feeling no fingerprints would be on that knife handle.

3

UNDERGROUND THEFT

WHAT WAS I doing in Sandy Pool? A Blaine Agency detective in a boom oil town? I'll get to that later. It had been important enough in the beginning. It was doubly so now.

For the time being all I could do—all I wanted to do—was stand around and watch the wheels turn. Jack Davidson was dead. I couldn't help him now, but I might get an idea.

Within fifteen minutes an excited crowd was around the little frame building, Moss, the deputy sheriff, was in the back room with Pete Younger.

The deputy was a burly man, with a close-clipped brown mustache, a shiny star and a cartridge belt, holster and gun under his coat. He swaggered in importantly and grew more important as he asked questions. After one look at me, and hearing I had just got in from Kansas City, he paid little attention to me. Which was all to the good.

Before he was through, the sheriff arrived with a car full of men from the county seat. Five minutes of the sheriff; and I saw why Pete Younger had dismissed him half-contemptuously as "old man Harker."

County politics and serving writs just about exhausted the sheriff's possibilities. He was a lank, gray-headed old fellow with a drooping tobacco-stained mustache, and a habit of drawling an idiotic observation and then looking wise while he waited to be agreed with.

"Looks like someone had it in for him," he commented, after walking around the body and studying it for several moments. "Doc, what's your verdict?"

"Doc" was the fat county coroner. He stood up and scratched his ear. "He was stabbed to death," he decided. "It's murder."

And while I choked off a groan of disgust, old man Harker addressed his deputy petulantly.

"Joe, I'm gettin' tired of all this trouble here at Sandy Pool. Gives the whole county a black eye. Can't you do something? It won't sound so good next election."

So help me, that's what he said. And Moss, the burly deputy, scowled and said, "What do you expect in a place like this? I'm doing all I can, but I can't keep an eye on everybody here, day an' night."

The coroner held an inquest there on the spot. The sheriff, his Sandy Pool deputy and two more he had brought from the county seat, muddled around with questions. As soon as we could, Pete Younger and I climbed into an old touring car, with the top down, and started toward the landing field, where boundary lights burned all night long. Oil men were using planes a lot, Younger told me.

He was considerably quieter as he talked.

"City detectives are out of my line," he said bluntly. "Oil fields are all I know, an' snooping around with a spy glass to see who did what never struck me as much. If we have trouble, usually we put out some men with guns and see that it don't happen again. If there's a killing, the sheriff and his men do what they can."

"If they don't have any luck, then what?" I cracked.

THE LANDING FIELD was just ahead. Behind us the night was red and eerie from huge gas flares burning free out of standpipes scattered through the maze of derricks. The stench of gas and crude oil was heavy everywhere. Drilling outfits working at top speed filled the night with a droning clamor of sound.

The automobile was lurching and jolting over a typical oil field road, which huge supply trucks had rutted into a shambles. That road would have given a Park Avenue chauffeur the screaming jitters. I knew that in daylight the field behind us would be a raw, dirty eyesore on the landscape, as grim, stark and efficient as the steel derricks and long strings of well casing.

But tonight, as Pete Younger spat over the side and steered the bucking machine with one huge hand, the strings of winking electric lights on the sides of the oil derricks and the gleaming rows of boundary lights around the landing field, gave the place a strange, unreal delicate beauty. Murder was the last thing the beauty of those thousands of winking lights against the night suggested.

Pete Younger's reply to my question had no more reality. "There's always something more coming along after a killing to keep everybody busy," he said. "If they can't find out in a hurry who did the killing, they're apt to forget about it pretty soon."

"Who's this Cass Cameron who was making threats today?"

We were abreast of the landing field. Younger turned off

the road toward the shanty at one end, where the planes stopped. A cold rasp came into his voice.

"Cass Cameron is the nearest thing to a dirty snake I've ever seen in pants. He's worth a million and a half anyway, and he made every dirty dollar of it by smooth lies, slick cheating, taking advantage of anyone who'd trust him, and plain thieving."

"Quite a man," I came back.

Younger misunderstood.

"Man, hell!" he snorted. "I told you he was a snake! He got his start selling fake oil stocks to widows, orphans an' any fool who'd believe his rosy promises. One day a dry hole they were putting down to make good on a lot of stock they'd sold hit by accident. I've heard tell the shock of having some crude oil to sell was almost too much for Cameron. But, after pulling a big drunk, he got used to the idea and decided maybe he could make more money out of actual wells. But he couldn't stop being a sharper. He's pulled every dirty trick in the book, including murder. And it looks now as if he's tried murder again."

"You think he came through that window and stabbed Davidson? And that Davidson let him?"

"Hell, no! Cass Cameron wouldn't risk his skin that much. But he's got money enough to hire a thousand killings if he needs 'em—an' there's a hundred men in Sandy Pool right now who'd take his money and do it," Younger said bitterly.

"What was his quarrel today?"

"I don't know," Younger confessed. "But I can guess. We've been having trouble with him. He pulled a crooked deal on an old blind farmer, and got some land next to our leases. Told the blind guy he was representing us, and got the old coot to sign papers he couldn't read, and his wife was too dumb to understand. Cheated the old man out of his eyeteeth. Then Cass Cameron started offset drilling against our wells, and when his first well missed the edge of the underground oil pool, he drilled his next wells at a slant, so they cut over into our sand a couple of thousand feet down and hit our oil. I drilled into a string of his pipe by accident, and got onto his game. Jack tried to stop him with the law, but the law's a tricky thing, and Cass knows every loophole. He's held us up on technicalities and gone drilling over into our leases. He's set to steal a fortune from us. Understand it?"

"I think so," I said. "His wells start all right on his land, but with the pipe going down thousands of feet, he can slant the bottom clear over under your land."

"That's right. A smart man can put the bottom of his pipe a quarter of a mile over to one side of the spot where it starts at the top of the ground. He can sit there over worthless ground with a pious look on his face, and steal the other man's oil a quarter of a mile away. That's what we're pretty sure Cameron is doing. But he's also trying to beat our wells down to the oil sand under our leases. Oil is funny. It lays there in the porous rock with heavy gas pressure over it. The first pipe down in that area taps the pressure. And what happens?"

"He gets the oil," I said.

Pete Younger cursed.

"He gets too much of the oil. As soon as he starts taking oil from one spot, the pressure around that spot gets lower, and the gas pressure over the whole area starts pushing all the oil around there toward the spot where that pipe is gobbling out the oil. So when the real owner of the oil finally gets his pipe down near there, his oil is moving over and going somewhere else. It just don't have any enthusiasm about changing its flow and coming back to the owner's pipe which arrived too late. First man down, first served. And Cass Cameron is trying to get his crooked wells in ahead of our wells each time."

"Can't you drill as fast as he can?" I asked.

WE WERE PARKED then beside the boundary lights of the landing field. The car creaked as Younger spat over the side again. In the faint glow of the lights his black-bearded face was stormy once more.

"Fast drilling," he said, "is made up of one thing an' another. A good drilling crew works together like a machine. When things go wrong, they don't work so well or so fast. When men get slugged in the dark an' knifed in the back, an' cable gets cut an' rotary drillers have things happen to 'em, all work slows up. The men don't know what's comin' next. One thing an' another so much has happened to my drilling crews lately, an' to my supply trucks, that my men aren't working worth a damn. Some of them have quit. I'll take my oath some of the new men I've hired are getting money from someone else to slow us up."

"Cass Cameron?"

He cursed again. "Who else? The more Cameron slows us up, the more he beats us into our own oil sand. He's takin' big chances and spending a lot of money in dirty work to gamble for another fortune. If most of his leases are on worthless land, and he gets into our oil with a string of wells, he can pull out a fortune before we have a chance to do anything about it."

"Won't those methods work both ways?"

"Jack Davidson is a white man," Younger growled. "We grew up together. Jack got schoolin' I didn't, but when we met again in the oil fields we unloaded pipe together for awhile. When Jack made his first strike he sent for me. I've been with him ever since, in bad times and good. Hell, I poured whisky for him on the night young Jack was born. And I never knew Big Jack to do anyone a dirty trick. He's got to be sure now. That's why he sent for you. He told me if he can prove any of this dirty work on Cass Cameron, he'll let me go ahead and take the lid off of hell right back at 'em."

The big fellow drew a deep breath. "I don't know what he'll do about the boy being murdered," he muttered.

Some of what he told me I had already heard from Davidson, Senior, in Kansas City. Davidson had mentioned no names, preferring me to dig them out with proof myself, as he had frankly said. Now I understood more clearly why he had warned me my life might be in danger. It was a queer, dangerous situation, charged with dynamite, with violence and death mixed with the huge sums of money at stake.

But I was still hazy about some angles of it.

"If Cass Cameron is behind all this trouble, and is getting away with it, and having everything his way, why should he have had young Davidson murdered?" I asked.

"I don't know," Younger confessed. "If I knew what they talked about today, maybe I could tell you. Jack was getting pretty desperate. This was his first big job on his own. It meant a lot for him to have it go off without a hitch. Instead, everything went wrong. His daddy was set to lose a fortune maybe. Jack must have found out something, or hit on some scheme to crowd Cass Cameron pretty hard. And when Cameron heard about it, he got mad an' made threats. That's the way it looks to me. And then Cameron went off and thought it over, and decided to spike young Jack's hand by killing him. Ain't it plain?"

"Too damn plain," I said. "A man as smart as Cameron seems to be would think twice before he'd make a crude move like that."

"Well, who did it then?"

"I don't know," I said.

And Pete Younger cursed bitterly once more.

"We've got to find out, mister! I'll never sleep easy again until I pin that on the guilty man. What's a bunch of damned oil wells? Jack's daddy and me had drilled plenty others. We could have drilled more in other fields if we lost everything here. But the boy is something else. He—we can't get him back now. He's gone. And in a few minutes I've got to walk out there and face the one man in the world I never wanted to see hurt. I've got to take him to the body of his boy who was like my own son. I've got to tell him I was somewhere else when the boy needed me most. The one time in my life I should have made good, I fell down on the job. Oh, hell!"

I let him bolt out of the car alone—off into the blackness of that windswept prairie alone. The drone of airplane motors was pulsing through the night, but I sat there in the car while Pete Younger blundered off alone. When a strong man's heart breaks and he blubbers helplessly like a kid, he wants to be alone.

And, dammit, I wanted to be alone, too. My eyes were damp also.

4

FINGER OF GUILT

THE PLANE WHICH came out of the northeast night was a fast, twin-motored cabin job. It circled the field once, and swooped down with floodlights glaring from underneath the broad wing, and landed neatly.

Pete Younger strode out ahead of me as the cabin door opened. Davidson was the first out. He was a tall, lithe man with a touch of gray at the temples, and a youthful alertness. Tonight his face, with its close-clipped mustache, looked as gray as his gray flannel suit, and tired.

They didn't say much, he and Pete Younger, who towered over him. Their hands clasped a second longer than customary, and Davidson said, "I'm glad you're here, Pete."

"You made a quick trip, Jack," Younger said gruffly.

"I ordered the fastest plane available."

The pilot followed Davidson out; after him came a young man, who turned and helped a young woman down.

She was young, pretty, stylishly dressed. She scuffed her shoe in the dust and glanced down with a flash of annoyance, and then looked toward the light-spangled oil derricks and made a face at the smell.

The young man gave her an annoyed look and turned to Pete, Davidson and myself.

Davidson said, "Phil insisted on coming along with his sister. Anne will go back with me. Phil will stay here and do what he can in Jack's place. He knows the routine here pretty well now."

"Good. I'll need someone in the office I can trust," Pete Younger rumbled with relief. "Harris, meet Phil Babcock, Mr. Davidson's nephew. You two'll be workin' together in this, I guess."

He was slender, this Babcock, and dressed like a Broadway playboy. But his thin face was weatherbeaten, and he gave me a handshake that mashed my fingers, and a keen stare.

"So you're a detective?" he said, and I didn't like the way he said it. He didn't think much of detectives or didn't like the way I shaped up.

So I said, "Here in Sandy Pool I'm interested in leases, when my name comes up."

"I'll remember," he promised, smiling, and left his sister out of it. She was dimpling at the good-looking pilot, as if she had just dropped in to see the sights. Her uncle's trouble wasn't weighing much on her mind.

I made the jolting ride back to the office with them. A crowd was still lingering there. They went in, and I followed. I had an ace up my sleeve.

Did I say Sandy Pool was running day and night? It was galloping at night.

The short main street was a few hundred yards over from the Davidson field office. I had an idea what I'd find, and I found it. Hastily erected wooden buildings were jumbled together on both sides of the street—two so-called hotels, saloons, new stores, lunchrooms, office rooms.

At the end of the street was a row of little one-room cribs, with girls waiting in the dim doorways. From an open window at the side of one building came the click of dice and murmur of voices. Huge, blundering trucks were trundling in both directions. The sidewalks were filled. Everything was wide open for business.

Why not? Drilling day and night, they were rushing down new wells as fast as pipe and supplies could be trucked in. Wages were high. Shifts were never stopped. The feverish feel of money was in the very air. Men slept in relays, as few hours as possible, and spent the rest of the time on their feet, trying for more of the easy money or spending what they had where they could.

ANY PLACE BUT those dim little rooms at the end of the street might have what I was looking for. And in the Palace lunchroom, adjoining the Palace Hotel, I found what I wanted. I was at the back end of the counter with my nose in a cup of coffee when a biting voice behind me said:

"Are you drinking that or bathing in it?"

Yes, it was Trixie Meehan, the slickest girl who ever signed an agency payroll. I had suggested that Trixie get to Sandy Pool a day ahead of me, grab off a job where she could look and listen without any visible connection with me. Before I left New York, Trixie had been sent from New Orleans. And now she breezed past me toward the kitchen in a soiled uniform with her arms loaded with dirty dishes.

But she was back in a minute looking for trouble.

Don't know Trixie Meehan? Then you'd swear she was a dainty little feather cuddled in flower petals; sweet, demure, and helpless. Strong men go giddy when Trixie lifts her long lashes and opens up those big blue eyes. One look and you see her so little, so cuddly, so fluffy—but if you stop there you've never met Trixie.

Behind that innocent little face Trixie can out-think all the wise boys. She left all her nerves at finishing school, picked up endurance that could wear me out, and polished it off with a diabolical temper and razor-edged tongue. But what a little trouper Trixie Meehan is on a case!

Now Trixie flounced out of the kitchen and slapped a damp rag on the counter before me. Her face was flushed, her blue eyes were snapping.

"I suppose, Ape," says Trixie under her breath viciously, "you thought this was a smart trick!"

"Is *this* any way to greet your palsy-walsy?" I gave her back. "In that dirty uniform you slay me, Sweetness. Did you get that egg on your chin off your plate, or from somebody else's dinner?"

"Mike Harris," Trixie choked, "I could boil you in the mess they called gravy tonight! There I was in a fine hotel in New Orleans, doing a society investigation, and you get me sent to this God-forsaken spot to carry dirty dishes and listen to cheap cracks from these oil field bums. *You* knew what you were getting me into!"

"Ixnay, here comes the boss," I warned, and lifted my voice for the Greek's benefit. "I'll have the apple pie and cheese, lady, if the pie's that good."

"Swell pie, mister," said the Greek approvingly, as he passed on to the kitchen.

Trixie got me the slab of pie and cheese, with a dirty look.

"Cheese makes me think of a rat," she said viciously.

"And a rat makes you think of me," says I, with a grin.

"Pretty stale. You're losing your snap, Angel. Got any dope for me? I suppose you've heard what happened to young Davidson?"

"Who in town hasn't been hearing about it?" says Trixie, tossing her little head. "They've been coming in here talking about lynching the man who did it. No one could be as nice as these roughnecks seem to think young Davidson was. And, according to them, his father is twice as swell."

"Which goes to show," says I, "that being a white man pays. But flowers won't help the boy now. We've got to find who planted that knife in his throat. It seems that will clear up everything else we're here for."

Trixie forgot her mad for the business at hand.

"I've heard several men hint somebody named Cameron might have an idea about it," she said, under her breath.

"That all?"

"Well," says Trixie doubtfully, "a little while ago a drunk made a crack to two men who were eating with him. He said 'It was a natural for him to get blamed for it, and before I'm through I'm going to have plenty.' I was clearing off the next table, and he had no idea I heard him."

"Good gal," says I, all ears. "What did he look like?"

Trixie jolted me with, "His friends went out. He's still over there at that third table against the wall. And I," says Trixie bitterly, "have to go back to the dirty dishes."

5

ANOTHER MAN DIES

THE MAN AT the table was oblivious to the clatter of dishes, the hum of voices. He sat there against the wall, marking with a pencil in a small notebook. So I took my pie to his table and used the old stall.

"Aren't you Charley Tillman I used to know in Spindletop?"

He wore dirty overalls. His stubble of sandy beard hadn't been washed since the last shave. His eyes were red-rimmed from lack of sleep. Squinting, he answered in a husky voice:

"I was at Spindletop, but you've got the wrong guy, buddy. My name's Jeff Hubbard."

"Well," says I, "it don't matter. I just got in. This looks like a live field."

He gulped some water, scowled at the taste, shrugged. "It ain't so bad. I'll get my stake here."

"Wages that good?"

He laughed shortly.

"Wages, hell!" Then he gave me a suspicious look. "What'd you say your name was?"

"I didn't. It's Harris," I gave him cheerfully.

"Got a job?"

"I'm on lease work."

He nodded idly. Lease hounds are a dime a dozen around any new oil field. He wasn't interested. In fact, he wasn't interested in me at all. Other things were on his mind. He was talking to kill time, and his eyes were constantly shifting to the front door, as if he were expecting something.

"How about a drink?" I suggested.

He refused with a surly shake of the head. "I'm tryin' to get my head clear now."

So I cracked, "Lot of excitement about that fellow getting stabbed tonight, isn't there?"

The sudden move his pencil made snapped the point against the pink oilcloth. He tried to look casual, and instead looked surly and on his guard.

Before anything more could be said, he saw something at the front of the room that made him shove the cheap little notebook into an overall pocket, and push back his chair.

"My head hurts too much to bother much about what's going on tonight," he said. "I'm turning in. Hope you make out all right, mister."

"Same to you," says I.

And when he left me I turned in the chair and saw a girl in a blue suit and a pert little hat going out the front door. Even at the length of the room I could spot the heavy makeup on her face, the cheapness of the loud blue suit and little hat. It wasn't hard to guess she lived down at the end of the street in one of those dim little rooms.

She hadn't been in the place when I came in. She lingered a moment outside the door, looking back. Trixie was dealing 'em off the arm as I made for the cash register with my check. Trixie flashed a look at the front door and kept her face straight, but I knew she hadn't missed anything.

The girl had moved off to the right. My man went to the right. And I eased out the door a moment later and went to the right also.

IT WASN'T HARD to pick them up in the crowd jostling along the sidewalk. She was walking a few paces ahead. Hubbard was trailing her, paying no attention to one who might be behind him.

They turned up the next side street, and he caught up with her. Dimly ahead of me I could see their heads close together as they walked slowly on. They stopped, parted, he went on and she turned back toward me.

And I was out on a limb. I wanted to follow Hubbard, and I didn't want her to spot me. He was already turning to the right down the next street. If I crossed over to the other side of the street I'd probably lose him.

So I kept on straight ahead, whistling nonchalantly between my teeth. She used strong perfume, and plenty of it. She was a few inches taller than me, and she looked hard at me as we met I thought for a minute she was going to speak, but she didn't.

When I turned the next corner I looked behind. She was silhouetted against the light glow on the main street, standing there looking back at me.

That wasn't so good. But at least she wasn't following me. I kept on.

I said Hubbard turned down the next street. It wasn't much of a street yet. Only a spot on the prairie, where passing trucks and wagons had beaten out a rough road. Shacks and tents had been hastily erected on it. Light came from a window here and there, and the night was murky red from the great gas flares and lighted derricks.

We weren't the only ones along here. Across the street a radio was blaring in a shack. Half a block back a woman was arguing shrilly with a man. I passed two shadowy figures on my side of the street, heard three men walking on the other side talking loudly. But my man kept straight ahead as if he knew exactly where he was going and was in a hurry to get there.

He went past the last house. The first oil derricks were not far beyond when he turned into a storage lot filled with oil well supplies.

And I was stymied. He might be merely cutting through that storage lot. He might be waiting close to the walk where he could recognize me if I passed. So I ducked away from the walk also, past the ghost-gray canvas of a lighted tent, circling back into the night past several shanties until I eased noiselessly into the storage lot.

There was enough light to show piles of well casing, stacks of timbers, five or six trucks parked there for the night. The shadowy quiet spot seemed to drowse there near the pounding activity of the oil well derricks. I had picked up a short, heavy stick on the way. I eased in past a pile of timbers, wondering if I had lost Hubbard and was playing the fool now.

Past the lumber to the left, beyond two parked trucks, a match flared for an instant between cupped hands and was extinguished.

Three or four minutes—fifty odd feet of ground—put me beside a big truck. Hubbard and another man were on the other side of the truck, talking in low voices. Hubbard's husky tones had a threatening note. The other man was merely murmuring.

Then Hubbard spoke a bit louder, irritably. "Take it or leave it. If anybody figures I'm afraid, they're due for a damn big surprise."

The reply was a dull monotone, without emotion. "You're tough, aren't you?"

Hubbard sneered then. "I'm plenty tough when I have to be. So what?"

The three shots which answered him were muffled, as if the gun muzzle might have been buried in cloth and flesh. But to me on the other side of the truck those shots tore the night apart. I knew that tonight another man had died.

6

MIKE HARRIS CHOOSES DEATH

MY AUTOMATIC WAS in my traveling bag at the Davidson field office. This gun had sounded like an automatic also. It would have more cartridges in the clip. I was a fool, and I knew it, as I ducked around the end of the truck toward the spot.

And I got my second surprise right there. He was coming my way. We crashed together right behind the truck. Sometimes I hate to be so small. His weight knocked me reeling into a sharp metal edge on the back of the truck.

Dizzy, half-conscious, I slammed the club at the cursing figure swinging around at me. He grunted with pain an instant before his gun roared in my face.

The blow spoiled his aim, or he was too startled to judge what he was doing. Twice he fired. Twice the crashing shots deafened me. And he only hit the metal truck body behind me as I ducked and swung the club again.

This time I missed. He was dodging away, vanishing in the night like a long-legged ghost. Then I realized I was hurt. The back of my head felt as if it had been torn open. I was sick, dizzy, unsteady on my feet. There wasn't a chance of catching him in this condition.

So I did the next best thing, and staggered around the

corner of the truck, and almost fell over the body I knew was lying there.

Already men would be running toward the spot. I didn't want to be caught here. But I had one thing to do and I did it.

Hubbard was inert as I groped in the dirty overalls for the soiled notebook I had seen in the lunchroom. I got it—and warm, wet blood on my fingers, too.

Men were shouting nearby as I left him there, left the club, and bolted. The gunman had gone toward the back of the lot. I went that way also.

The voices were out in front. Others were coming from the rutted street where Hubbard and I had walked. I went out of the back of that storage lot, to the left, like a rabbit bolting from a brush pile.

Fifty yards ahead was a cross street of sorts, with scattered shacks along it, facing the street. Two men ran out of the shacks. I dropped to the ground as they headed into the storage lot. Skirting one dark, shed-like little building, I waited beside it while men dashed past the front. And then I ran out and followed them.

In front of the storage lot where the crowd was gathering I lingered a few moments, and then went on.

Under my hat the scalp was broken, bleeding, swelling fast. And hurting more every moment. But that didn't matter. I had the notebook. What did matter was the knowledge that I wouldn't know the gunman if I bumped into him under a bright light. He was a head taller than me. His voice had a queer expressionless monotone. Other than that he had been only a figure in the dark.

But if he had any brains, he'd know me again. A little

man like me should have been easy to notice—and should
be easy to pick out again.

WHAT LUCK I had still held. The shots had been heard all
over town. The crowd had deserted the Davidson office.
Sheriff, deputy sheriff and their men had rushed to the new
scene of trouble. I got to the office as an undertaker's hearse
from the county seat was just driving away. Inside were
Big Jack Davidson, Pete Younger and the nephew, young
Babcock. Gillis, the clerk, and Anne Babcock were gone.

They stared as I walked in.

"I understand there's just been a shooting," Davidson
observed heavily.

"I heard the shots," I said. "Where can I wash my
hands?"

Pete Younger took a towel off a hook. "There's water an'
soap an' a washpan out back. I'll show you."

I turned to follow him, and Phil Babcock said, "There's
blood on the back of your shirt collar."

"Is there?" I said.

"And your suit looks as if you've been crawling on the
ground."

"Does it?" I said, and turned back to him. "Mister," I
said, "is anything about me any of your damned business?"

His face got red. He started to bite his lower lip and
didn't. Instead he said:

"It certainly doesn't interest me, Harris. But on the other
hand, you're mighty touchy about two casual remarks."

I said, "My head hurts like hell, and I've got too much
on my mind to be bothered with fool remarks. If you make
'em here, no telling what you'll say in front of the wrong
person. Either I'm working without any buttin' from you

or anyone else, or I'm out of it quick. Let's understand each other right now."

Pete Younger put a hand reflectively to his bushy black beard.

Davidson frowned. "This is hardly a time I care to hear an argument," he said. "You took offense too quick then, Harris. But you're right. Phil, I suggest you don't interest yourself in what Harris is doing unless he asks for your assistance, or you find out something he should know. Then do all you can for him."

Babcock's face was still red. He didn't like it, but he shrugged.

"Gladly," he agreed. "I regret I annoyed you, Harris."

Out back I washed in a tin basin, while Pete Younger stood beside me, huge and shadowy.

"Davidson going back to K.C. tonight?" I asked him.

"Nope. He an' Miss Babcock are going over to the county seat tonight, and start home with the boy tomorrow."

"Man by the name of Jeff Hubbard was shot a little while ago," I said, wiping my hands.

Younger's voice rumbled softly through his beard. "Was that his name? Hurt him bad?"

"Killed him."

He was silent a moment. "Anybody got any idea who done it?"

"I haven't. I was there. Got my head hurt trying to stop the man that did it. He got away."

"Know why this fellow was shot?"

"I've more than a hunch it had something to do with young Davidson's death."

Younger stood there looking down at me and plucking at his beard.

"I wonder how," he growled. "Hubbard worked on my number three drilling crew until he quit, four days ago."

7

EVIL IN THE DARK

DAVIDSON AND PETE Younger went for a walk. It was easy to understand how Big Jack Davidson wanted to get away from this office into the night with his old friend. Babcock went out too while I sat at Gillis's desk and went through the little notebook.

Pete Younger had told me he didn't know a thing about Hubbard, except that the man had known well drilling, had gambled steadily, had quit without any reason.

One edge of the notebook was smeared with a crimson stain. Perhaps a quarter of the pages had been scribbled on with pencils at one time and another. There were names, addresses, notes, accounts, reminders.

See Shorty next week.

Jack LaGrange gen del Long Beach Cal.

Owe Ed 18.50—Owe Skinner 5.00—Lent Slim Edwards 10.00.

Mabel Pike swell baby.

Lia Drane 1050 Grant Tulsa Okl.

Those samples were in a scrawl almost impossible to read. Now and then he had put down the scattered notes of a hodge-podge diary. He had hitch-hiked from El Paso to Fort Worth. Before that he had been in jail for a month in Globe, Arizona. Those pages contained names of men he had evidently met in the jail.

One note at that point looked like pay dirt. *See Blick Barnes at Sandy Pool. Whitey says hello and I'm right guy— ask if anything doing.*

That sounded good. And then—*borrowed twenty Blick... ten Madge.* Then a page of figures, as if he had added daily wage totals.

That was about all on Sandy Pool. The last two pages, where he had been scrawling when I saw him, were a jumble of lines, letters and designs.

The door opened. Phil Babcock came in. I put the notebook in my pocket and stood up.

"When Younger comes back, tell him I want to see him before he goes to bed tonight, if possible," I said. "And if he knows a good place to sleep, I can use it."

"The Palace Hotel or Mrs. Claghorne's boarding house will take you in if you use our name. Try the Palace. Younger stays there, and I did while I was here before."

"Ever hear of a man named Blick Barnes?" I asked him.

Babcock shook his head. So I took my bag into the back room and changed my blood-stained shirt. Out back I had washed the blood from my hair, found the half-inch gash in my scalp had stopped bleeding, and decided to let it go until morning. The swelling was hardly visible, the pain was getting less.

Leaving the bag, I went out with Blick Barnes on my mind. The automatic was under my arm this time. They were playing too rough in Sandy Pool for carelessness.

In the Palace lunchroom Trixie served me another cup of coffee, and under her breath venomously gave me:

"I'm dying on my feet, Simon Legree. I'll hold this against you the rest of my life. What about that man you followed out?"

"Him? Oh, he's dead."

Trixie gulped. "Was *he* the one that was shot?"

"No less, Sweetness."

"Mike," said Trixie faintly, "did you—"

"Be your dirty dishes! But I was in at the execution. Almost got a piece of it myself."

Trixie drew a breath of relief.

"A nitwit like you shouldn't be allowed out after dark alone," she gave me bitingly. "*What* are you going to do next, Mike Harris?"

"Heard anyone mention a chap named Blick Barnes?"

"No."

"Keep your ears open. Ask a few questions from the other hashers in here. I'm also looking for a girl named Madge."

"What kind of a girl?" Trixie asked suspiciously.

"She probably won't be slinging hash."

"Which goes to show," says Trixie bitingly, "what the rewards of virtue are. I'm going off the job in fifteen minutes, Useless. I'm staying upstairs in the Palace Hotel, next door. The same Greek owns it. Two other waitresses here have the same room. 217. It's a little worse than steerage."

"But think of the tips," says I, tossing a nickel on the counter and leaving before Trixie could unlimber her tongue.

FROM THERE ON I hit a blank wall on Blick Barnes. Every casual question I dropped in likely spots up and down the street drew blank. I looked for the girl who talked with Hubbard, and didn't see her either. I caught Younger at the field office and asked him about Barnes. No luck there. Babcock made the score perfect.

"The deputy sheriff was back here and I asked him if he knew Barnes. He hadn't heard of the fellow," Babcock volunteered.

So I took my bag to the Palace Hotel and asked for a room. The young Greek at the plank counter gave me a rathole at the end of a second floor corridor. He swore by Athens it was all he had, and only Davidson's name got it for me.

The raw frame building hadn't even been painted yet. Somebody was constantly entering or leaving a room. But I sorted out what little I knew, what I had to do in the morning, and dropped off into uneasy sleep.

It had been a wild evening. I had the feeling this isolated little hell-hole on top of a lake of oil was going to be wilder for me, before I left. And, some time in the dead of night I came abruptly awake, sweating coldly.

8

A KNIFE IN THE DARK

I SLEEP ON a hair trigger. Agency work encourages that knack. Now I came awake in that dark little cubbyhole certain something was wrong.

The night was still black. Through the open window at the head of the bed I could see out to the lighted derricks, where moving machinery rumbled and clanked. The room itself was pitch-black and quiet as death as I lay there with nerves taut.

Downstairs a radio was playing. Men were talking. A cash register rang faintly. And the sickish odor of cheap perfume crept into my nostrils.

I couldn't see her. She might have been a foot away, or six feet. But I knew she was there in that black, death-like quiet. And only murder could have brought her here, in the night, to my bed.

A floorboard creaked right beside the bed. A solid chunk of blackness bent forward toward me, and I hurled the sheet and blanket at it and rolled off the bed to my feet.

She was fighting the covers off her face and arms when I grabbed her. She twisted like a cat and struck at me. A knife point grazed my shoulder. I got her arm with one hand, got the wrist with the other hand, and twisted her arm against the fulcrum of my right arm.

She moaned once. The knife fell to the floor, and we stood rigid in the darkness, panting. Every move had been as silent as the death which had come to Jack Davidson.

"Maybe," I gritted, "you made a mistake and got in the wrong room!"

"Leggo my arm, damn you!" she gulped. She was crying.

I should have yelled for the clerk downstairs. Instead, I dragged her over, reached up for the light cord and turned on the light.

She wore the same cheap, blue suit, pert little hat, raw makeup. She was a young, cheaply-pretty girl, sullen now, red-eyed, frightened, and defiant as she fiercely gulped:

"All right, yell for the sheriff, you lousy killer! Gawd, I—I wisht I'd brought a gun instead of a knife!"

A red crimson patch was growing around a small slit on my pajama sleeve. She had dropped a thin stiletto capable of slicing through a man's chest with one push.

"Sit in that chair," I told her.

"I ain't afraid. Go on and get it over with," she sneered.

So I cracked, "Sit down, sister, before I slam you down."

She knew that kind of talk. She sat. And I said, "What's your name?"

"Chase yourself," she gave me, dabbing a crumpled handkerchief at her nose.

So I got cigarettes, tossed her one, held a match. Her hand shook as she inhaled and stared up sullenly.

"Who sent you here, Madge?" I tossed her casually.

She sneered again, "Wrong guess, you lousy little dick! Madge ain't the name an' nobody sent me. I just wisht to Gawd I'd brought a gun."

"All right, you wish you'd brought a gun," I agreed. I drew on my own cigarette. "Why?"

"You know damn well why!" she flared. "Didn't I see you followin' him? Don't I know you kilt him? The only guy who ever gave me a break an' ast me to marry him—an' you shot his guts out before I had a chanst to ever get a home an'—an' kids of my own."

"So?" says I. "Who was going to give you all that?"

"*You* know who! Jeff Hubbard."

"What makes you think I shot him?"

"Didn't I see you sneakin' after him?"

"But that," says I, "don't mean I shot him."

"You ain't kiddin' *me*. I know what I know."

"How do you know I'm a detective? How did you unlock this door—and how did you know I was in here?"

"Gawd, I wisht I'd brought a gun!" she gulped.

"Give me the key you used," I snapped.

SHE HESITATED, SHRUGGED, fished it out of a pocket. Plain, cheap locks were in the doors. This key had a different style than the hotel was using; an ordinary skeleton key that would work in most locks of the type.

"I suppose you know my name?" I suggested.

She shrugged.

"Asked at the desk, eh?"

She shrugged again.

So I said, "You figured I killed your boy friend, so I was due for the same?"

"You had it comin', damn you! The only guy who ever give me a break, an' you hadda knock him off."

"And your name isn't Madge?"

"What if it isn't? What's anybody named Madge got to

do with this? Go on, turn me in an' see how much I care," she sniffled, wiping her nose again. "I don't care what kind of a break I get now."

"Your boy friend was going to meet someone else when you left him, wasn't he?"

"I ain't admitting nothing. Go on an' waste your breath if you get a kick outa it."

"Suppose I told you the fellow he was going to meet shot him?"

"Think I'd believe that? I got the straight of it!" she shot back.

And I had what I wanted. She wasn't acting—not with that yarn about a home and kids. She wouldn't have brains enough to use that for an excuse if it weren't the truth. The man who had shot Hubbard had tipped her off I did it. And that I was a detective.

"I didn't shoot your boy friend, sister. Take it or leave it, whichever way suits you. I just got into town tonight. If you're wise, do a little thinking and figure out who did get him. Now scram out of here and let me get some sleep."

"You mean—get outa here after—after—"

"Scram," says I, "Maybe I'm a better friend than you'll ever know. Maybe I can help you if you need help. Think it over. I'll be here tomorrow."

She sidled toward the door, staring at me, as if waiting for me to change my mind. She had the door open six inches, still watching me, when she decided it must be true.

"Okay," she said through dry lips as she started out. "Maybe I'll see you again."

So I fixed the slit in my arm, locked the window, propped a chair under the doorknob, and went to sleep again.

9

BEAUTY—AND A SINISTER BEAST

THE TOWN LOOKED different in the morning. It was twice as active, raw, ugly, and no longer mysterious. Here was company; here were men on every side intent on their business. It was hard to believe the events of the night before really had happened.

Big Jack Davidson had departed, leaving word with Pete Younger for me to hire any help I might need, to spare no expense and hesitate at nothing to find out who had killed young Jack.

Why hadn't I tried to follow that girl in the night? Because I wanted her to wonder also why I didn't follow her. I wanted the next move to come from her—or from whomever she was dealing with.

Sure, it might mean another knife or a handful of bullets. Blaine Agency cases aren't always taffy on a stick.

After talking with Pete Younger I went to see Cass Cameron—and found him watching one of his drilling crews under a tall steel derrick.

He was a handsome fellow, about three inches short of six feet, wearing polished tan riding boots, a thin sport sweater and a cream sombrero. Neat as a pin, freshly shaven, thin-faced, smiling. He looked down at me as if I were a long-lost friend.

"Yes, I'm Cameron," he said. "Can I do something for you?"

"Yes," I said. "Let's get away from this machinery and talk about young Jack Davidson."

His face didn't change. His smile didn't drop a degree in warmth. But an opaque curtain rolled down behind his eyes, as he nodded without hesitation and turned to leave the well platform.

But I knew as I climbed down with him to the dry, sandy soil that big, bulllike Pete Younger hadn't told half the story about Cass Cameron. Here was a man I'd be as much afraid of in daylight as in dark. He was so clever I was certain my flash of instinct had been right. The best way to deal with Cass Cameron was to tell the truth. And I'll tell you why later.

A dozen paces away from the derrick he turned to me with little sun and humor crinkles radiating from the corners of his eyes, and said:

"You know, Harris, you're not the first person this morning who's come to talk about young Davidson. I wonder if you have the same idea some others have—that I know something about his death?"

On my oath, he said it amiably; and continued to smile easily as he watched me. Not a word about who I was, what business it was of mine. As deftly as a fencer flicking back a blade he put my question back in my face and waited with amusement for the answer.

So I smiled too and said: "What do you think?"

He chuckled. "Sometimes I wonder if I think at all," he said.

Like that he answered me without effort—told me nothing—and still asked no more as he waited, smiling.

"You don't stack up to all I've heard about you," I said. "And just between us, I'm going to get confidential. I'm a detective, Mr. Cameron. I'm trying to find out who killed Jack Davidson—for his father, of course—and I'll lay my cards out before you. I've heard it suggested you know who killed Davidson. In fact, with just a little more proof, a warrant will be issued for you."

HE SHOULD HAVE been in the movies. He merely lifted his eyebrows slightly. His smile didn't change. Even I was not sure I wasn't imagining the trace of puzzled uncertainty with which he searched my face.

"I've heard," he said, "that even a little proof is often hard to get. I appreciate your frankness. Is there anything I can do for you?"

So I grinned at him.

"Not that I can think of at the moment," I said. "I just thought I'd let you know. Glad to have met you."

The smile was frozen on his face as I left him. It wasn't, I thought as I went back to the main street, a bad start at all for the day. I was thinking of the mysterious Blick Barnes, when I saw Trixie Meehan emerging from a store entrance just ahead. She stopped there on the walk, was peering into her vanity mirror when I said:

"All bright and cheerful this morning?"

"I'd be cheerful if I could forget dirty dishes and you," says little Trixie coldly. "What interesting visitors you have in the middle of the night."

"Did you see that girl?"

"I'm not interested," says Trixie bitingly.

"There you go exploding about nothing again," I came back heatedly. "That dame almost stuck a knife in me."

"Indeed?" says little Trixie sweetly. "The next time you tip me a nickel I'll be tempted to do the same."

"What do you know about her? What were you doing up so late watching my room?"

Trixie tossed her head.

"I was sitting in the lobby, keeping my eyes and ears open, when I saw her walk in. I recognized her as the woman that that drunk and you followed out last night. She went upstairs. I trailed after to see what room she had.

"Imagine my confusion when I saw her easing into your room like an old friend," says Trixie scathingly. "My room is just down the hall. I left my door ajar until she came out with a cheery promise to see you again. Suppose we drop the subject?"

"You get in my hair with your wisecracks!" I yelped.

"Maybe *that* woman will interest you also," Trixie sniffed, looking at a woman who swept out past us, followed by a colored woman loaded with packages.

They went to a big, cream-colored Cadillac sedan parked at the curb. And I forgot my peeve as I stared at beauty which must have tamed the beast. She was a shade taller than Trixie—about my height. Her hair was fine and gleaming black, her skin was milky white, and her features were strangely suggestive of an Oriental. In this boiling boom town she stood out like an orchid in a ditch, as she slipped behind the wheel and sent the big car spinning down the street, trailing dust.

I fumbled for a cigarette. "Now *that*," I murmured, "is some ornament for Sandy Pool. I wonder who she is."

"Why not look her up?" Trixie said sarcastically. "You wanted a 'Madge,' didn't you? That's Chinee Madge, who does the hostessing for Lon Thompson's Sandy Queen Inn. Thompson heads our thriving little underworld, I understand; and Chinee Madge is one of the most notorious women of the oil towns. She's Lon Thompson's girl, by the way, if you feel a romantic urge."

10

MURDER KNIVES

SOMETIMES YOU SWEAT for an idea and miss it, and then it flies up and hits you between the eyes. Chinee Madge, Lon Thompson, the gambler, and the Sandy Queen Inn were like that!

Trixie had heard her customers talking about Chinee Madge, had dropped questions, had spotted Chinee Madge's well-known cream-colored Cadillac parked in front of the store, and had gone in herself to see what Chinee Madge looked like. And then I came along.

The Sandy Pool underworld was little, but thriving. Lon Thompson was its king. The Sandy Queen, down at the end of the street, occupied the second largest building in town, and was doing the biggest business.

Ostensibly the Sandy Queen Inn was a place to get a drink, dance with your girl, or even eat in the booths around the dance floor. Actually the Sandy Queen offered anything from knock-out drops to loaded dice. I found music and a crowd inside. The bar was doing a rushing business; the dance floor was full; and in a long side room that made an L-turn across the back of the building, the gambling games were wide open—roulette, birdcage, dice, faro—anything you wanted.

Chinee Madge's big car was parked outside. I had a drink at the long bar, wandered through the gambling room, heard some big poker games were going upstairs, and watched for Chinee Madge.

Finally I spotted her coming down wide wooden stairs from the upper floor. She was talking to two oil men. Through tobacco smoke and bad jazz from an amplifying phonograph I saw her smiling faintly, as a Chinese woman might smile, revealing nothing. At the bottom of the stairs she nodded, said something, and turned away with the same faint smile.

I caught her just inside the gambling room.

"Didn't Jeff Hubbard owe you ten dollars?" I asked.

The breath of a frown etched between her black, arched eyebrows. "Did he?" she said. "Who are you?"

"The name," says I, smiling, "is Harris. And I'd like to pay off Jeff's debt if you're the lady."

"What did Hubbard say?" she gave me, smiling faintly.

"He said," says I, thinking fast before her quizzical look, "that he'd had to borrow ten from Madge and twenty from another fellow. And then he went out and got himself shot."

"You must be quite a friend of his."

"I owe Jeff a lot," I told her, with the shadow of a sob in my voice. "Maybe I can even up a little by squaring his debts. Good old Jeff. I wish I knew who shot him."

She nodded, and said, "Jeff Hubbard returned the ten dollars. I'm afraid you've wasted a good deed."

By then I was sure she had Oriental blood in her. She was as slim as Trixie Meehan, perfectly shaped, delicate as a bit of Chinese porcelain. Her voice was clear, low, pleasing.

"Good deeds are never wasted," I chuckled. "I've met you, haven't I? And while we're talking, maybe you can give me some idea where I can find Blick Barnes?"

Sure, I was rushing matters, taking chances, risking a lot on the slip of a tongue. But too many cross-currents were running in Sandy Pool; too much was happening from hour to hour to waste any time. Hubbard's little notebook had given me an edge on the game, and I was pushing my luck hard.

The faint smile stayed on her face. "What do you want with Blick Barnes?"

"I want to pay him twenty dollars for Jeff, and ask him some questions."

She said, "Perhaps Lon Thompson can tell you where he is. Lon is around somewhere."

I FOLLOWED HER into the gambling room. The man whose arm she finally tapped was watching a dice game.

"Lon," she said as he stepped aside with us, "this is Mr. Harris. He knew Jeff Hubbard, and he's looking for Blick Barnes."

Lon Thompson was chewing a toothpick. His lean jaws kept moving as he stared at me from a pair of cold gray eyes.

"What's your business with Blick Barnes?" he questioned slowly.

He was past forty; his face was long, lanky, broken by a short black mustache and slashed by a scar from the bridge of the nose to the cheekbone. The cold eyes had a lazy droop as they stared at me. But lazy or not, it took a tough man to hold down a tough place like this.

"The lady asked the same thing," I told him. "Have you

got Barnes hidden away somewhere? I'm regular. Hubbard would have told you that."

"He's not here," Thompson said evenly.

"That's why I'm asking you."

Thompson nodded slowly. He shifted the toothpick to the other side of his mouth, then took it out and glanced at the frayed end.

"Blick Barnes ain't in town today," he said idly. "Come back about dark and I'll take you to him."

I was passing the bar on my way out when I met Pete Younger coming in. Funny how a thing will strike you suddenly. The big fellow wore the same overalls tucked in muddy boots, the same weatherbeaten sombrero cocked over one eye. His bold-nosed, bearded face was no different—and yet, somehow, he managed to look embarrassed.

"Haven't seen young Babcock in here, have you?" he asked.

"Is he supposed to be in here?"

"Never can tell where a man'll be," Younger muttered. "Had any luck?"

"Not much. I saw Cass Cameron."

"Found anything against him yet?"

"Not yet."

Younger cursed under his breath. "Cameron came over to tell me he'd heard talk that he'd killed Jack. He said that the talk was wrong—an' when I gave him half a minute to get off our leases, he told me he was shootin' in an offset to our number nine well this evening. He's beat us down by ten days easy, an' I'll bet his pipe's over in our sand. Hell, I hope you have some luck soon."

Younger went back toward the gambling room. And a

few moments later I eased back after him. I was just in time to see him going upstairs with Lon Thompson. They were talking like old friends.

Pete Younger had evidently lied to me about coming to look for Phil Babcock.

"Now why," I asked myself as I went out, "did he do that? And how-come he's so thick with Thompson?"

And then I left the place wondering how that girl last night had been so sure I was a detective. No one but the elder Davidson, Pete Younger and young Babcock had known that. Not even Gillis, the clerk, unless some of them had talked in front of him.

I DIDN'T KNOW her name or where she hung out. And I was wondering what she was going to do, if anything, when I saw something in the cluttered window of a small store which sent me inside.

The place stocked a little of everything, from overalls and shoes to hardware and canned goods. Two clerks were busy with other customers. The man who came forward to wait on me looked like the proprietor, and was a German.

"You've got some knives in the window, behind those overalls," I said.

"Sure, you vant a knife?" He reached into the jumble of goods in the window and got a small cardboard box of knives.

"Are they any good?" I asked.

He looked hurt behind his spectacles. "Dese knives," he swore, "are de best shteel, mister. From Chermany."

"You're not selling many. Only two are gone out of this box."

"Ach," he said. "But one of dose knives I sell to Mr. Cameron, de big oil man. He knows goot shteel."

"You don't say," says I. "And who bought the other knife?"

He shrugged.

"His name I cannod tell you. But I see him in de Sandy Pool Company's office. He shtoop a little undt his hair is yellow."

"That's good enough for me," says I, and I bought a knife and walked out, wondering what I'd stumbled on. The knife which had been in Jack Davidson's throat had come from the box half-hidden in the cluttered window. And Gillis and Cameron had bought the only two knives sold from the box. Which one had killed young Davidson?

11

THE THIRD KNOCKOUT

GILLIS WAS CHECKING some reports when I walked in. His sharp face was almost as sallow as his hair; he looked ill and nervous this morning.

"Not worrying, are you, Sweetheart?" I asked, throwing a leg over the edge of his desk and staring at him.

His tight mouth pressed together. He frowned at me and said coldly, "I don't feel well. Get off my desk, please. I'm busy."

"Sure," I said, and stayed where I was. "I'm looking for a knife. Got one I can borrow?"

He pulled out a drawer and handed me a penknife.

"Too small," I said. "Haven't you got one about this size?" And I tossed the bone-handled knife onto the desk.

He stared at it with a kind of horror. When he looked up his eyelids were blinking, his mean little mouth was working nervously. "I—I don't understand. If you have a knife, why—why try to borrow one from me?"

"I'm peculiar that way. Sure you haven't a knife like this one?"

His Adam's apple bobbed in his throat as he gulped, "I—I've got one in my room."

"Let's go get it."

We went without any argument. Gillis walked beside me as if in a daze—which was queer, since the knife we were after would put him in the clear.

Gillis drew a deep breath and spoke to me as we walked. "Where did you get your knife?"

"Bought it the same place as you did yours."

"You act like a detective."

"I am, if it makes you feel any better."

"I thought so," he said, half to himself.

And I pounced on that. "Did you tell anyone what you thought?"

"No," Gillis deified woodenly. "I don't have much to say to anyone."

That was all he said until we stepped on the narrow porch of a long, unpainted, frame building which looked like a temporary army barracks. An enormously fat woman with pink curl papers in her hair was standing on the porch, giving orders to a colored girl. She beamed archly at Gillis and wheezed, "My, I hope you ain't home for dinner already, Mr. Gillis."

Gillis gave her a sickly smile.

"No, I'm not here for dinner, Mrs. Claghorne," he denied, and led me through a long hall to a little pigeon-hole bedroom at the rear. A cot, a chair, some nails driven into the wallboards comprised the furnishings.

Two locked suitcases stood beyond the chair. Gillis's hand was unsteady as he unlocked one of the suitcases and fumbled inside.

"Here," he said, tossing a rolled shirt over on the cot. "The knife is inside."

"Then don't be so shaky. You haven't anything to be

afraid of," I said, and stooped over the cot and unrolled the shirt....

THE NEXT THING I heard was the wheezy, excited voice of the landlady, saying, "He was just like that, I ain't got any idea what happened. Ain't that blood on his head?" For the second time since I had hit Sandy Pool the back of my head felt as if it were coming off. I was weak, groggy, sick again, as hands rolled me over, not too gently.

I was still in Gillis's room, on his cot; and Joe Moss, the burly deputy sheriff, was bending over me. The fat landlady was behind him, and several men were crowded inside the doorway behind them.

"What happened to you?" Moss demanded, as he helped me sit up.

"Where's Gillis?" I groaned.

Mrs. Claghorne wheezed: "I have not seen Mr. Gillis since you two come in here this morning. I didn't think nothing of it when he didn't show up for his dinner—and then Marthy unlocked the door to leave a fresh towel an' found you lying here like a dead man. I didn't smell no booze on him neither, Mr. Moss."

My wrist watch showed ten minutes of two. I had come in with Gillis about ten-thirty. Tie that.

"Didn't you see Gillis go out alone?" I asked her; and she sniffed and said indignantly, "Indeed I did *not!* I got too much to do running this place to stand around and watch the front door. Where is Mr. Gillis, is what I want to know? He ain't never missed a meal since he came with me, until today."

"The door was locked, wasn't it?" She had the backs of

her hands on her billowing hips and she was belligerent now. "I said so, didn't I?" she snapped.

Gillis's suitcases were still there. Screen wire tacked outside the open window was still in place. He'd gone out the door all right. I touched the back of my head and winced.

The deputy sheriff said accusingly, "The back of your head's hurt, hey? Had a fight with this man, didn't you? Come on, now, what happened?"

"Gillis slugged me," I said. "I'll sign a charge. He's probably out of town now. Better check at the office."

"What'd he slug you for?"

"Maybe his hand slipped," I snarled. "I'm not under arrest. Don't make a grandstand play over me. Search his suitcases and get word out to the sheriff's office to catch him. Davidson will back me up, if that means anything to you."

Davidson's name did the trick. I sat on the cot and smoked a cigarette, and damned my carelessness, while Moss went through the suitcases. What a sap I was to let Gillis slug me from behind. But then how could I expect anything like a vicious slugging done with cat-like quickness by a worm whose hands were still trembling when he seemed on the verge of clearing himself from any suspicion.

His shaking hands should have warned me. But even now I couldn't see how Gillis could have been fool enough to stab Jack Davidson with a knife bought locally, and then leave the knife in his boss's throat while he calmly typed outside the door until the body was discovered. I ask you.

The suitcases contained only clothing. Gillis had taken with him the blackjack or gun he had used on me. But not my gun, nor my money. Gillis had decoyed me to his room, slugged me, locked me in, and slipped off light-handed and ready to travel fast and far.

THE DEPUTY HAD the landlady lock the room again and walked to the Davidson office with me.

"Mister," he said darkly, "the way you're covering up on this looks mighty funny. Didn't you have an argument with him?"

"Get him and I'll talk to you," I said.

Phil Babcock was at the office in an ill humor. "Have you seen that fool, Gillis?" he snapped at me as I walked in.

"We're looking for him," Moss blatted importantly. "Gillis knocked this man unconscious at Mrs. Claghorne's place and disappeared. I want him."

Babcock said weakly, "Knocked *you* unconscious, Harris?"

"I'm ashamed to admit it, but he did."

"I'll be damned!" Babcock commented. "Gillis! Now, why did he do that?"

Moss complained, "This man won't tell me why. But he says Mr. Davidson will back up the charge. I guess you know about that, hey?"

"He don't and he won't!" I snapped. "Gillis must have hopped a truck or taken an auto out of town; maybe a plane. Find out what you can, but get word out first to stop him."

Young Babcock was looking at me queerly. He still seemed dumfounded.

"Gillis," he muttered. "I wouldn't have believed it." And then he came out of it and spoke curtly to the lingering deputy. "Get Gillis if you can. This is apt to be pretty serious."

The deputy left, muttering to himself. It was easy to see what he'd like to do to me. But that was his worry.

"Did Pete Younger find you?" I asked Babcock.

"Was he looking for me?"

"I saw him in Lon Thompson's place this morning. He said he was looking for you."

Babcock burst out angrily, "Damn his nosy curiosity! I'm getting damn sick of him!"

"Why?" I asked.

And he snapped at me, "Last night you shot off your mouth about people minding their own business! Try a little of it yourself now!"

Well, I had *that* coming, but what was this between Pete Younger and Babcock now?

The rest of the afternoon I had more than that to think about. Gillis had simply vanished. It wasn't hard to do in the furious activity and hodgepodge of strangers in Sandy Pool. Hardly anyone knew anyone else; strangers were arriving and departing all the time. Gillis hadn't gone out on a plane. I checked that myself.

Jeff Hubbard's death was still unexplained. Trixie hadn't seen Hubbard's girl yet. And by that time I remembered the man who had killed Hubbard had been long and lanky like Gillis. And Gillis had been away from the office about that time. Could he have killed Jeff Hubbard also? And if so, why had he done it?

12

A WILD RIDE

TRIXIE SLAPPED A water glass on my table and snapped, "Did you hibernate all afternoon?"

"I was unconscious part of the time."

"You usually are, aren't you?" says little Trixie scathingly. "I had news for you, and couldn't find you."

"Get it off your chest," I yawned, lifting the water glass. "But this case is practically in the bag, if what seems correct is correct."

"About one-thirty, when I got off after the dinner rush, I saw your last night's girl friend go into the Davidson office," says Trixie.

I choked in my water glass. "Who was she talking to?"

"A young man who looked like your description of Mr. Davidson's nephew."

"I was in there after that. He didn't say anything to me about her."

"He probably thought you were still unconscious," Trixie said helpfully.

"What did they do?"

"Talked—and then she came out and hurried to the Sandy Queen Inn. When she went in, she looked determined. When she came out she seemed upset and in a hurry."

"Then what?"

"I had to get back to work in a little while, so I left her in Thompson's place and looked for you. And did I find you? What are you eating tonight?"

"Nothing," says I, getting up. "Shuck that apron, tuck your gun in your purse and get over by the Davidson office in case I need you."

And I charged out through the twilight to catch Phil Babcock before he left the office. He was typing temperishly on Gillis's typewriter when I came in.

"What about that girl who was in here this afternoon?"

"What girl?" he asked, hoisting his eyebrows.

And I blew up. "Don't stall. What did she have to say?"

He got to his feet. He was pale. "What business is it of yours to whom I talk?"

"Plenty! That dame broke into my hotel room last night and tried to put a knife in me. She went with Jeff Hubbard, the fellow who was shot last night. What were *you* doing with her?"

Pale? He was white as a corpse. His teeth clamped over his lower lip as he stared at me. In that moment, he hated me wildly. I set myself for trouble, but he controlled himself and spoke in a strained, stiff voice.

"I haven't anything to say to you, Harris."

"Where's Younger?" I snarled.

"I don't know."

"Think fast while I get him!" I blazed, turning to leave. "He's apt to knock loose your stubbornness. I hope he does."

Babcock was biting his lip hard as I slammed the door. Trixie was loitering in the dusk at the corner.

"Babcock's in there," I threw at her as we met. "If he goes out, follow him. If you see Pete Younger, identify yourself, tell him what you told me about Babcock and the girl, and tell him Babcock won't talk to me about it. I'll be back shortly."

Trixie nodded, turned away, and I went on. Trixie was like that when action was needed—cool, and hard as steel.

I went to the Sandy Queen Inn after this mysterious Blick Barnes, to see what I could blast out of him about Hubbard's background in Sandy Pool. Too many things were tracing back to Hubbard. Too much mystery was centering around this fellow. And Blick Barnes, the man Hubbard evidently first saw in town, should have most of the answers.

NIGHT—THE WEIRD FLAME-LACED night of a new oil field—was dosing down when I entered Lon Thompson's place. The crowd was already standing two deep in front of the bar. Thompson didn't seem to be around.

A plug-ugly bouncer beside the dance floor told me Thompson was gone. I asked for Chinee Madge.

"Look upstairs," he growled.

So I looked upstairs, along a wide hallway where doors standing ajar revealed poker games inside; and she came out of one of the rooms and arched her black eyebrows and said, "Back again?"

"Didn't you think I'd be?" I countered, grinning while I watched her face. I was wondering how much she or Thompson had heard about me from Pete Younger or Hubbard's girl.

Her faint smile showed only mild amusement.

"I'll have to drive you," she said. "Lon had to go out on some business. Do you mind riding with me?"

"Should I?" I said, and she chuckled low in her throat; and I chuckled. She said, "My car's outside. The cream Caddy. I'll be out in a few minutes."

When she joined me she wore a black coat over her black silk dress. She backed the big cream-colored car around like an expert, eased it down the street, turned to the right past the outlying well rigs, and drove fast along a rutted dirt road.

"Where are we going?" I asked.

"Barnes is staying with a friend several miles out this way," she said, without turning her head. "If I go too fast, tell me."

The speedometer needle was already above sixty. On that narrow dirt road, cut up by heavy traffic, the big car swayed and slammed like a bucking bronc. Inside of a mile I was cold with fright. That slender, delicate little Chinee Madge was driving like a mad woman. In the dashlight glow a faint smile of contentment was on her face as she wrestled the bucking wheel. Now and then she slammed on the brakes and made a weaving, skidding, heart-stopping turn, only to pick up speed beyond it.

Now and then we passed a big truck or an automobile heading toward Sandy Pool. The country on both sides was wild, desolate in the bobbing beam of our headlights.

"How far is it?" I asked.

"Not far," she answered, without taking her eyes off the road—and the next instant I went against the windshield as we skidded into another turn.

I came out of that with a small handkerchief my grop-
ing hand had found down behind the seat. I dropped it,
put a cigarette to my lips—got a whiff of my fingers—and
grabbed the handkerchief again and smelled it.

Jeff Hubbard's girl had left her handkerchief there
behind the seat. Her rank perfume marked it. The crumpled cloth was still damp as if the owner had been crying
into it very recently.

"What's the name of Jeff Hubbard's girl?" I asked as I
shoved the handkerchief in my pocket.

"Did he have a girl?" says Chinee Madge calmly.

"Don't they all?"

"I don't know her."

"I thought I saw her in your car this afternoon?"

"I haven't had a woman in my car today," she answered
calmly.

And I wondered then how much of a devil she really
was; how vicious, how dangerous, and how much I could
trust her on this trip we were making into the lonesome
night.

SHE SLOWED DOWN, turned to the left onto the twin
shallow ruts of a ranch road. The headlights glanced over
a fresh black-and-white sign which warned: NO TRES-
PASSING—DANGER.

"What's the danger?" I asked.

"Explosives. A well shooter lives there." She laughed
softly. "We may meet his truck along the road here. I
understand he's shooting a well tonight. He'll be taking
the nitroglycerine in as soon as the worst of the traffic gets
off the road."

The back of my neck prickled. Long cans of nitroglycerine are sometimes lowered to the bottom of the well casing and a weight is dropped down on them. The explosion shatters the oil rock for a great distance around, so that the oil rushes freely to the bottom of the pipe.

The well shooter has to keep that nitroglycerine around somewhere, has to transport it over treacherous roads to the oil wells. If you know nitro, you know the slightest jar will sometimes set it off. When a nitro car blows up they never find the driver. He simply dissolves over the landscape.

And I wondered where Chinee Madge had learned a well was to be shot this evening. From Pete Younger or Cass Cameron? I wondered why she had lied about Jeff Hubbard's girl, who—according to Trixie—had been badly upset when she entered the Sandy Queen Inn. I wondered just why I was being taken out here.

I wondered so much I reached over, cut off the ignition, and took the key from the lock. "Let's talk this over," I said. "It looks like a plant to me."

Chinee Madge stopped the car so quickly I almost went through the windshield again. She grabbed a purse off the seat beside her and had her hand inside by the time I got back on the seat and snatched at her wrist.

13

OILY LIQUID DEATH

SURPRISE? SHE FIRED the gun in that purse right through the leather at me. The bullet went roaring between us, into the back of the seat.

Using both hands, I jammed the purse down into the seat between us as she fired again, and then I got one hand into the purse to her thumb, and twisted the thumb until she let go of the gun.

Surprise? Have you ever been massacred? I was massacred right there in that car seat. That slim, controlled little Chinee Madge exploded into a murderous, fighting hellcat beside me.

Her sharp fingernails raked my face, tore at my eyes. She bit, cursed, kicked—and tried to get at her gun again. In the dashlight glow I saw her hand flip down to a garter band and come out with a little, vicious dagger.

I chopped up under her arm, drove the blow aside—and fifty seconds later had her disarmed. I always carry thumb cuffs. They're handy. I cuffed her thumbs together, drove the car well off the road, into a hollow, and then locked her arms around the steering post. When I tried to question her she blistered my ears, so I said, "I'll walk ahead and see for myself."

She was still swearing when I closed the door and limped back to the road, dabbing blood from the scratches on my face. Surprise? *Never* again, I hope. The car windows had been closed. I hoped no one had heard the shots.

Miles off into the southwest I could see the lurid glow of Sandy Pool. Starlight was all I had to walk by, but it was enough. Half a mile farther on I topped a rise of ground and saw a lighted window ahead.

I was almost to the house when I made out two cars and a small truck parked there. Light from the nearest window showed the small, panel-body truck painted red. Its sides were lettered: DANGER—EXPLOSIVES! This was the nitro truck. A voice was audible in the small frame house. I eased to the side window, looked in—and almost swore aloud.

Gillis was sitting in there. Lon Thompson was standing in front of him. Two other men, wearing bib overalls, were sitting. Gillis was tied and gagged. Thompson was saying, "That's the best way, Simpson. Take 'em both in your truck."

Simpson needed a shave. He had a broken nose and a cauliflower ear. His reply sounded surly. "That's more than I bargained for, Thompson."

A gasoline lamp lighted the room brightly. Thompson's face scar was livid from the bridge of his nose to his cheekbone: His voice was a dull, threatening monotone.

"Don't give me that, this far along in the game. They're both going in the truck. The sheriff's looking for Gillis. He'd be the first man to tell you to arrest him."

Simpson stirred uneasily. "Maybe so, but I don't like it."

Thompson looked at his watch, "I've got to leave here

in about five minutes if that punk don't show up by then. Whitey'll see you don't change your mind."

I'D BEEN ON the point of starting for the front door. It looked like Thompson was ordering Gillis taken back to the sheriff. Everything law-abiding and right, despite Chinee Madge's actions. But Whitey, stocky and muscular in his bib overalls, said, "Don't worry, Blick; he'll do it."

This Whitey evidently was the man who had steered Jeff Hubbard to Blick Barnes. Lon Thompson was Blick Barnes—and he had just spoken in a monotone I'd heard before. Chinee Madge had been bringing me out to this lonely place like a lamb to the slaughter.

But why were they sending Gillis back to the sheriff? I dodged away from the window as the nitro truck creaked. Something had moved inside that truck. Gun out, heart hammering, I listened—and heard a choked sob inside the truck. The sounds stopped as I opened the rear doors. "What's the matter?" I whispered.

A woman groaned. Her head was just inside the doors. My hand found a gag, found her hands tied. I risked the split-flare of a match. She was Jeff Hubbard's girl!—and, by the way her eyes widened, I knew she recognized me.

She was almost incoherent when I got the gag off, and I was sweating. I'd caught a glimpse of padded compartments on the floor holding slim metal cans half as long as a man. They were merely cans—but each one, I knew, was filled with many quarts of oily, liquid nitroglycerine. A few spoonfuls of the stuff could tear the door off a heavy steel safe. My insides crawled when I thought what the quarts and gallons of the stuff in those cans could do.

I pulled her out, cut the ropes from her wrists, led her off into the night where we could talk. She was still trembling.

"I was scared to death in there with those cans!" she gasped. "Jeese, let's run before they get us!"

"They won't get you again," I promised. "What are you doing out here? Did you tumble that Thompson shot your boy friend?"

"How'd you know?" she sniffled. "I—I got thinkin' that if you didn't shoot Jeff, maybe Thompson did. And maybe, when I told Thompson I'd seen you followin' Jeff, that was why Thompson said you sure did it, and egged me on to go after you."

"Let's see," says I. "You came to the lunchroom and got Hubbard that night."

"Uh-huh," she whimpered. "Jeff told me to tell Thompson to meet him out somewhere private for a talk. Thompson had had Jeff throwed out of his place the day before, because Jeff quit his job an' went on a drunk. Jeff wasn't having any more of that."

"Why did Hubbard want to see Thompson?"

"I dunno. But Thompson had been payin' Jeff to do dirt where he works. Jeff told me that."

"What were you doing in the Sandy Pool Oil Company's office this afternoon?"

"Jeese, you know *everything*, don't you?" she whimpered. "I told Thompson maybe he shot Jeff, an' he laughed at me an' said he had a dozen men who'd swear he never left the Sandy Queen last night, an' he'd have me run out of town if I didn't watch out.

"So I got mad an' went to the Sandy Pool office an' told the man there just how Thompson had been payin' Jeff—an' other men too—to do dirt at their wells. An' he told me to tell Thompson I knew that, an' see if Thompson wouldn't let slip why he done it—an' if Thompson did, it was worth a thousand dollars to me."

"So like a fool you went back and tried?" says I.

"Mister," she gulped, "I needed that thousand. Thompson wasn't there. His girl gave me a drink that musta been doped. When I woke up she was drivin' me out here. I tried to jump out. She pushed a gun in my side. An' when I got here, the men tied me up an' put me in that truck."

The house door opened just then. Thompson stepped out. His voice was plain. "I'll be waiting at the Queen for you."

He drove off. I left the girl there, went to the house window, then to the front door, and charged in with my gun out, yelling, *"It's a pinch!"* And the next instant I had to shoot, as Whitey's hand snatched a gun from an overall pocket.

14

THE NITRO TRUCK

I DRILLED HIM through the arm. He dropped the revolver and backed off, holding the arm and swearing wildly. Simpson's hands were in the air. He looked stunned. Gillis made queer noises behind the gag, and then toppled off the chair in a faint.

"Come on in, it's all right now!" I yelled to the girl. She came to the steps and stayed out there. I searched Simpson, found him unarmed, and made him ungag Gillis, who was coming out of the faint.

"Thank God you're here!" Gillis babbled, sitting on the floor.

"Don't be so hasty," I advised. "You're going back to the sheriff just the same. And I may slug you for luck on the way. Make a sucker out of me, will you?"

"I hardly knew what I was doing," Gillis moaned, "I'll be glad to go anywhere with you. At l-least I'll have a chance of living. These men were going to tie me in the seat of their nitro truck, stop it out on the road, blow it up with a time clock, and then drive to the sheriff in their other car and say I and—and some girl stole the truck after dark, and tried to escape in it—and blew the truck up by our reckless driving!"

"They *will* play rough, won't they?" says I. "Did they teach you how to slug from behind so neatly?"

"I never saw them before!" Gillis protested wildly. "I—I went to Thompson and told him my predicament, and he put me in the back of his car and brought me out here. And then he came back a little while ago and had me tied up, and stood there and planned what to do with me. It was ghastly."

"So you went to a crook like Lon Thompson?"

Gillis moaned. "Thompson had found out some way I was sentenced for embezzlement some years ago and escaped. He threatened me with that, and offered me money for copies of our office records, our geologist's reports, drilling records and plans from day to day. I had to do it. And so when I had to have help, I went to him."

"And got what you deserved, you mealy-mouthed rat!" I told him. "Did you, by any chance, hold out anything that passed between Cass Cameron and Jack Davidson when they quarreled yesterday? Don't tell me now you weren't listening."

Gillis gulped.

"Mr. Davidson told Cameron he had found out that Thompson was furnishing men to sabotage our wells, and that he was going to go over the sheriff's head to the governor and have Thompson run out of Sandy Pool, and also going to arm men and stop action on the Cameron leases until they found out whose oil he was getting. And Cameron told him he couldn't get away with it."

"And Cameron also warned Davidson he'd get the surprise of his life if he tried it?" I finished. "Where did you go after you bought that knife?"

"I stopped in Thompson's place to drop some reports, and then went home. I—I've wondered if I didn't lose that knife there," said Gillis, thoughtfully.

And I said, "Well, we'll see. Get up. Do what I say. If you didn't kill Davidson, you've got a chance for your life. If you did, and pull one funny move with me, I'll shoot first and talk later. That goes," I snarled at the other two, "for you also. You, Whitey, wind something around that arm. All of you get out to that nitro truck. Make it snappy. I'm in a hurry."

BEFORE WE STARTED I cuffed Simpson and Whitey together with my other pair of thumbcuffs, ordered them inside the truck, and snapped the strong padlock which was hanging on the rear door for just that purpose. Gillis and the girl rode in the front seat with me. A wooden panel cut us off from the prisoners. Leaving them to ride as best they could I started for town.

There was no sign that Thompson had found Chinee Madge. I left her there with her sins, and picked up speed. Soon muffled yells of protest began to come from the two prisoners in the truck.

A jackrabbit couldn't have bounced wilder over the prairie than that red-painted little truck did as it skittered and plunged over the rough road toward town. Fists hammered on the panel behind me; I heard Simpson bawling wild oaths of alarm, and I only drove faster.

The light-spangled derricks, the leaping red gas flares and the lights of Sandy Pool grew brighter, and we rolled past the first derricks, and I turned down the outer street and drove the back way to the office. It was lighted. Through the window I could see Pete Younger and Phil

Babcock talking. Younger opened the door when I blew the horn.

"Get the deputy sheriff and bring him to Thompson's place!" I called.

"Moss is probably there right now himself. He usually is. What the devil are you doing with that truck?" he yelled, grabbing at his black beard. "Ain't that Gillis?"

"It is. Send Babcock for the deputy and come along." And I started the truck with a lurch as soon as he stepped onto the running board.

"Watch out, you fool! Want to blow us all to hell?" Younger bawled.

"You should have seen us coming to town," I gave him, and rolled fast to the front door of the Sandy Queen and stopped. "Watch everything," I said. "I've got a couple of prisoners in back. I'll be out in a minute."

And I hustled inside Thompson's little hell hole and pushed through the crowd, looking for Thompson. The first man I saw was Joe Moss, the deputy sheriff.

"Seen Thompson?" I asked him.

"He went past here a few minutes ago," Moss said sourly.

"Come along and help me find him. I've got some business for you."

Scowling, he tagged after me—and back in the gambling room I found Thompson talking to Cass Cameron. Talk about luck! But then almost anyone in town could be found in there sometime during an evening.

Cass Cameron lifted his eyebrows at me. "Making progress, I hope, Harris," he smiled.

Thompson smiled too. He looked like the cat that had

stolen the cream. "I thought you were going to look me up this evening, Harris."

"I'm looking you up now," says I. "Come out in front a minute. You too, Cameron. Maybe this'll interest you."

"What kind of a stunt are you pulling?" the deputy growled at me.

"Come see," says I.

THEY CAME, PAST the bar, through the front door, through the small crowd that had gathered about the truck. When Thompson saw the truck, and Pete Younger standing there with Gillis and the girl, he stopped like he was shot.

"Wh-where did *that* come from?" he squawked.

I jabbed my gun in his back and pushed him forward.

"I found this truck standing in the road a few miles out of town," I said. "Gillis and the girl were just getting out. They had some fool story about having been tied in the seat on your orders, and left there to be blown up. They claimed they had just gotten loose. Younger brought them in in his car, and I drove the truck in here to get the straight of it from you. Do you know anything about it?"

"Of course not!" Thompson almost shouted. "Get that damn truck away from here! It may blow up any second!"

"Why should it blow up! Stand still!" My gun in his back stopped him.

"You'll tear this whole end of town off the map if it blows up!" he said wildly. "Moss, do something!"

Moss said, "What's wrong with it now?"

Cass Cameron had a queer, uneasy look on his face as he stared at Lon Thompson. The crowd was beginning to murmur.

Thompson's teeth began to chatter. "I don't know anything about it, but I won't stand here!" he burst out wildly. "Moss, this man is insane! Get him away from me!"

"We'll stay right here," says I, "until we find out what's what about this cock-and-bull story."

And then Thompson went crazy. He tried to swing around and grab my gun. I slugged him to his knees.

"You can't do that!" Moss protested angrily.

"Stay out of this!" I snarled. "This is the man who killed Jack Davidson! I'm going to get the truth right here!"

Thompson tried to struggle up. I shoved him down. His nerve broke then. He screamed, "Get me away from that damn truck! Gillis is right! There's a time clock in there set to fire that nitro! It's hung up someway, but it's liable to go off any second! Get me away from it!"

No man could doubt his raving admission. Men were knocked down and trampled as the crowd broke and scattered. Even Cass Cameron went. Only Pete Younger's long ape-like arm kept the deputy from fleeing. Thompson tried to get up. I shoved him down again.

"You did stab Jack Davidson with the knife Gillis bought, didn't you?" I threw at him.

"Yes, what of it? Let me get away from here!" he gasped, trying to get up again.

"Why'd you do it?" I said, slapping him back with my gun barrel.

And he moaned, "Davidson had made plans to close up my place. I had too good a thing here, and in helping Cameron, to lose out. Last night I went to the back window, beckoned Davidson to it, let him have it, and pulled the shade down and went on! Is *that* enough for you?"

"What did Hubbard want last night?"

"He saw me at the window and tried to blackmail me!" Thompson blatted out hysterically, and came up fighting to get past me, away from the truck. Pete Younger grabbed him and held him while I said:

"Take it easy. There isn't any nitro in that truck now. I had it all unloaded."

IN THE SEVERAL minutes it took to convince him, men were still leaving the building by windows and doors, quickly had the word spread. And when Thompson got the straight of things he almost collapsed.

I mopped my forehead. It had been some strain. "That was one time a bluff got me something," I grinned to Pete Younger.

And the big fellow rumbled disapprovingly at me, "Son, from what I hear of that ride in, it was one time you had the luck of a fool. Simpson is half crazy inside the truck there. In the dark he missed one little quart can of nitro when you made him unload, an' he says you drove so fast he an' the other feller in there was floundering all around that can. He thought it was going off every second."

Then my hands began to shake.

"One little quart can of nitro?" I bleated. "B-back in there all the time, and I didn't pay any attention to their yelling?"

And Trixie Meehan spoke weakly at my elbow. "Mike, you are the *biggest* fool."

"Where did *you* come from?" was all I could say to her.

"I followed Babcock here. When he ran, I stayed. What's the matter with your face?"

"A woman scratched it."

"You'll learn," says little Trixie disgustedly.

And with that quart can of nitro on my mind I could only nod agreement.

THE LETTERS AND THE LAW

*A Stack of Letters Worth a King's Ransom
Hurl Mike and Trixie into a Knock-Down-
Drag-Out Brawl with the Toughest Cutthroat
Mob on the Whole of the Florida Coast!*

1

IN THE RING –

MIAMI LOOKED THE same—white clouds in the clear blue sky—the February sun bright and hot—when I tipped the Pullman porter and dashed through the station to a taxi.

"Geigler Building on Flagler Street," I panted at the hacker.

"Nice weather we're having," he beamed as he closed the door.

I was mopping perspiration off my face and neck. "Terrific!" I groaned. "What I need is an oversized ice plant."

"Ha-ha—it is a little warm today, isn't it?" he burbled over his shoulder as he drove off. "But think of the weather they're having up north."

"If I think, I'll melt," says I, shoving my heavy overcoat over on the seat and mopping perspiration.

He thought I was kidding him. I don't know what Bradley's office girl thought when I walked in on her, still mopping perspiration.

"Why, it's Mister Harris!" she squealed, hopping out of her chair.

"Hello, Dotty," says I. "Last spring it was Mike, wasn't it?"

"It's going the wrong way, Mike!" Trixie protested

"Dotty?" says she, cooling off. "Don't you even remember my *name?*"

"Could I forget it," I remembered just in time. "Prudence, the little lady who couldn't forget her name."

"I thought we agreed to forget all that," she reminded with sweet charity.

"Pay no attention to me," I cracked. "My meter isn't connected yet. Where is Bradley?"

She reached for the phone. "I'll tell him you're here."

"Is he in conference?"

"Why—why, yes and no," says Prudence. "I think he's expecting you; just let me tell him you're here."

"Never mind; I'll tell him myself," I refused, starting toward Bradley's door.

"Don't argue! Come on!" I yelled, half-dragging her along

"Really—" Prudence protested weakly.

But I was already opening Bradley's door....

Maybe you've never met me—Mike Harris, of the Blaine Agency. I'm red-headed, five feet and a shadow, and life doesn't seem much more than one case after another. I've got a vacation coming—but I'll give you that later.

Bradley was behind his desk, lighting a fresh cigar.

"I'm here, thanks to you," I snorted, tossing the overcoat on a chair and peeling off my coat and vest.

"So I see. You're a sight for sore eyes, Mike!" says Bradley heartily. He came around the desk and grabbed my hand. "I'm certainly glad to see you, Mike. Yes, sir, I certainly am."

Bradley managed the Miami office. He was gray-haired and immaculate, smooth as a Junior League smile and hard-boiled as a dowager's determination. Just the man for that stretch of gold coast between Jacksonville and Miami. Bradley could soft-soap a chair full of jittery millions or strong-arm a gold-washed crook with the same finesse.

"Never mind the greeter's lullaby," I handed him sourly. "Where's your ice water? Where's a fan? I'm burning up."

Bradley chuckled. "It isn't *that* hot here, Mike."

"Meet this sun in an overcoat, a winter suit, winter underwear and socks, and then sing your song," I retorted. "Those ditherwits in the New York office didn't care whether I had on earmuffs or rubbers when they wired me to change trains at the next junction and get down here. Dish me the dirt before I melt on your floor."

"It's a woman," says Bradley, returning to his chair.

"Isn't it always?" I cracked, drawing ice water from the cooler in the corner.

Bradley took the cigar from his mouth and sighed. "But what a woman, Mike!"

"So was Eve, and she took the apple."

"In this case," Bradley informed me wryly, "the lady plants the tree, too. Give this Lucille Palmer a brace of free tickets to an opening and she'd leave with the show."

I tossed the paper cup into the waste container and surveyed Bradley. He was deeply affected; more so than I'd ever seen him.

"It must be pretty bad," I said. "Give me the worst. This Lucille Palmer sounds to me like a great discovery."

"In a way she is," Bradley admitted ruefully. "I've met some sharp-witted women in my day, Mike, but I don't believe I've ever seen one who could stay in the money with her. Yes, she's a discovery."

"So was Little America—but what does one do with

it? What has the lady done—tampered with your happy home?"

"I," said Bradley severely, "am a very moral man, Mike. But Colonel Wedgewood, the beet-sugar king, unfortunately forgot himself. It would be more truthful to say he lost his reason. Lucille Palmer led him back to the cradle days and made him beg for the bottle."

"So what?"

"So," said Bradley, "it's two hundred grand for the letters—or else."

I GAVE BRADLEY a vicious look. "Did you have me sent all the way down here to recover a sap's letters? Tell that peepshow grandpappy to pay off the lady and charge it to education."

"This," said Bradley earnestly, "is no ordinary case, Mike. You know me well enough to know I don't go off half-cocked when a client cries on my shoulder. Colonel Wedgewood has paid off already with jewels, cash, and a long list of expensive odds and ends."

"So now he's left with the odds while the lady keeps the ends? What does he want?"

"Forty-seven torrid letters," Bradley informed me sadly.

I yawned. "Don't you know," I asked wearily, "that if she's asking two hundred grand for those letters, he should tell her to take the squawk to the Supreme Court—or jump off the Hoboken Ferry? No one pays any attention to dirt any more. She couldn't get it into a New York court if she carried a union card. Where is he from?"

"New York and Denver. But a breach of promise suit is not what Colonel Wedgewood fears, Mike. His lawyers can handle that without difficulty. The old man is enough of a fighter not to care much what the newspapers print."

"Then who's crabbing about what?"

Bradley rolled the cigar in his fingers. He looked as sad as a corporation lawyer reviewing a bad case.

"Colonel Wedgewood gave me the complete picture," he sighed. "Relations between the colonel and his wife are strained—very strained. The colonel washed a great deal of the family dirt in those letters. He was in an agitated state of mind at the time; and he felt certain he had found a marvelously understanding girl who was happy to share his troubles and sympathize. So, in the various letters, he wrote it all out, with appropriate comments. If Mrs. Wedgewood's lawyers get hold of those letters, they'll bomb him with some of the things he put down. He'll be forced into a property settlement which will cost him several millions. And that, my boy, is not penny arcade money."

"You make it sound very pitiful," I said sarcastically. "The colonel will have only a couple of million left, I suppose? I could weep at such poverty. Why is he squawking about two hundred thousand if that much will save him several millions? He'll never turn up another deal that will pay him such a percentage."

"On the face of the matter, yes," Bradley admitted. "But Colonel Wedgewood is certain other demands will follow. He has no way of knowing that this Palmer woman won't keep photostatic copies of the letters—which would be quite enough for Mrs. Wedgewood's lawyers. You see, due to the facts the colonel put down in the letters, this Lucille Palmer is quite aware of the situation—and how valuable the letters really are."

"The man certainly went whole hog when he decided to play the fool."

"He couldn't have done worse," Bradley sighed again. "I don't see any way out but to get the letters, and at the same time make certain no photostatic copies exist."

"In other words, you want a miracle—so you send up north for me to do your dirty work?"

"It's an important and delicate case which must be settled quickly and carefully, Mike," Bradley pleaded earnestly. "I couldn't think of two people in the Blaine organization better fitted to do it than you and Trixie Meehan."

That blew me out of the chair yelping: *"What?* Trixie Meehan? Not on your egg-stained vest! I wouldn't work panhandlers' row with that little torpedo! Nix! *Nein!* No! Get it? *NO!* Trixie's raw-hided me for the last time! If you send for her, I take a runout powder and go back to New York. Do I make it plain?"

Bradley's face was red before I finished. He coughed behind his hand, looked distressed.

"Aren't you a little severe on Miss Meehan, Mike? You two have done some great work together. She's tops in her class!"

"So is prussic acid in its class!" I snorted. "I'm not having any of Trixie Meehan this trip—and that's that!"

Bradley coughed again.

"Unfortunately," he sadly informed me, "Miss Meehan is—er—"

"Miss Meehan is right here!" says a voice I know only too well. "And if that sawed-off little eohippus has any more cracks to make about me, I'll add up the check myself!"

2

THE PARADE

FROM THE NEXT room Trixie swept in—little Trixie, pert as ever—and primed for trouble. And I started back-pedaling fast.

"Am I surprised?" I bleated weakly. "You know—"

"I know," says little Trixie, glaring. "Don't soft-soap *me*, Numbskull!"

Never met Trixie Meehan either? Life has passed you by. Trixie is no bigger than a gadfly. But her blue eyes are so-o-o big, and soft and melting. Trixie's misleading little face has a way of making old men husky and young men weak. Trixie tripping by on the main stem is as soft and helpless as a bit of fluff on an autumn breeze.

But *this* Trixie, who worked Blaine Agency cases with me, was concentrated hell-on-wheels. Her cuddly curves had the strength of an adagio dancer, her fluffy helplessness masked a chilled-steel nerve, her mind clicked eighty to the minute, and Trixie's pink little tongue could take the skin off a chromium gargoyle. *What* a woman—and here she was loaded for bear.

"This *is* a surprise," I got out weakly. "Ha-ha, *what* a surprise. I didn't know you were below the Mason-Dixon line, Trixie."

"I'll bet you didn't," says Trixie.

So I let her have it back twice as nasty. "I took the pledge on you, sister, that last case out West. You're poison to me. You give me nightmares with that razor-edged tongue. I'm not having another helping, if you ask for it on a hot griddle. No more—get me?"

Trixie put her little hands on her little hips and cut me down with a look.

"I get you," she gave me coldly. "But since when were *you* heaven's gift to anyone, Ape?"

"Time!" yelled Bradley. "Call off this cross-country feud until you break this case! I've explained it to you, Miss Meehan. You've got the layout, Mike. The Palmer woman is registered at the Miami-Plaza. She's dealing through a New York law firm. I think they're shysters. One of the partners, a man named Louis Layre, is also at the Miami-Plaza. That's all the help I can give you. Now give me a little help. *I'm* the one that's in hot water here. It's my office that'll get the heat if the Palmer woman puts it over."

Trixie had calmed down. She gave me a nasty look and the lift of her shoulder, and spoke to Bradley. "Are there only two of them?"

"As far as I know."

"Only two," says Trixie demurely.

"That shouldn't be hard to handle."

"Now, listen," I said desperately. "I told you—"

"Of course," says Trixie sweetly to me, "if you're a cowardly quitter, Mike. If you're afraid of this Palmer woman—"

"Afraid of her? Me afraid of *any* woman?"

"Hmmmmm," says Trixie, giving me the up-and-up

under her long lashes. "Well, we'll see. Mr. Bradley, where is this lovely old sapodillo?"

"Colonel Wedgewood and his wife have opened their Palm Beach villa," Bradley explained hastily. "They're doing the social whirl rather big this winter. This Palmer woman has turned up with her squeeze just when it will be most embarrassing and damaging to the colonel's peace of mind and—er—his wife's good nature. That sent him to us so quickly and—uh—desperately."

"I adore desperate men," Trixie giggled.

I sighed. "I'll take the hook," I said. "But if a certain party gets in my hair I'll run her back to New York so fast her brogues'll smoke. And that's no maybe. Furthermore, *I'll* give the orders."

"Of course, Nitwit," Trixie agreed. "You always try, don't you?"

"Now there you go—"

Bradley waved us down. "The sky's the limit on expenses," says he hurriedly. "Colonel Wedgewood wants results. He's willing to pay through the nose to get them. Could anything be fairer?"

"Or sweeter?" Trixie sighed.

"We'll get results," I promised sourly. "But how he'll pay! Start the swindle sheet with a bottle of good Scotch. I've got to think."

"Dynamite might blast it out quicker," Trixie suggested helpfully.

Bradley stood up with a wild look in his eye. "Go into the next room there and plan it any way you like," he choked. "Only don't bite in the clenches."

Trixie saw my ideas—after an argument which brought

Bradley to the door twice. He didn't interrupt because we had the door locked. When we had it settled, I drew a check to the expense account that made Bradley gag, and took the next plane back to New York.

A day's hard work got me luggage, clothes, and a big, lean valet by the name of Bitters. From my room at the Pierre, I wired the Miami-Plaza to reserve a suite for Mr. Michael Harris and manservant.

THE NEXT DAY Bitters and I flew south. Just before dark we hit the crowded Miami-Plaza lobby like good news from home. You could hear the conversation gagging when I breezed in wearing a bright suit that screamed for attention, with Bitters, in ministerial black, towering at my heels, and four bellhops staggering after him with loads of swank luggage.

"Mr. Michael Harris," I gave the pop-eyed clerk. "I reserved a suite by wire."

He fussed with his necktie, opened and closed his mouth silently, looked at the bellhops ganging behind me, and said, "Uh—yes, sir! Uh—will you register, please?"

I waved my hand languidly up at Bitters.

"I won't," says I. "But my man will. Have me put in my suite quickly, please. And send up the manager."

Near me an over-dressed fat woman made a remark which cut through the sudden quiet.

"How odd!" she said.

I turned, saw her eyeing me through a pair of nose-glasses she held up with a pudgy hand.

"Bitters," says I coldly. "Make a note of anyone who shows interest in me."

"A note?" Bitters gulped, looking around wildly.

"You heard me. A note. A memorandum. I wish to be informed, you idiot, of the presence of any suspicious characters. Do I make myself plain?"

Bitters was breathing heavily through his nose by then. He barely managed to bleat, "Yes, sir. Quite so, sir."

By that time the lady had her glasses down and was breathing hard, too. "Well, I *never*—" she gasped.

"Madame," says I coldly, "you'd better." That got me into the elevator and up to the suite. There I handed each of the bellhops a ten-dollar-bill.

"Young men," I told them severely, "I want service. Very good service. I'm willing to pay for what I get. There's more where that came from. Pass the word along. Furthermore, I'll pay twenty dollars for a complete description and report of anyone who tries to pump the staff about me. Do I make myself plain?"

They were pop-eyed by then. The nearest bellhop stuttered, "Are you expecting a sh-shot in the back, Mr. Harris?"

"Son," I told him, "I'm expecting the manager just now. Get him up here."

They did.

The manager was a pudgy, pink-faced man who looked as if he could suavely handle any situation which might arise about the hotel. But he entered the suite warily; and he grew fidgety, and his eyebrows went up when he heard my demands.

"I want four bodyguards while I'm here," I told him coldly. "Big men. Competent men. The uglier their faces, the better. Put two of them outside my door immediately. And have the other two waiting in the lobby every time I come down. Day or night. On second thought, you may need more than four to keep that schedule."

He moistened his lips.

"That, Mr. Harris, will run into quite a sum of money."

"Did I ask you about money? I want the guards."

That sank him. He looked at me with askance. His thoughts registered on his face. He was wondering if I was a big shot dodging trouble up north—and expecting a blow-up down here. Miami, of course, was the happy playground of the big money crooks from all over the north. But usually they buried their differences and lived in harmony while they took the sun and planned future business.

My request for guards was making the manager wonder if I wasn't one of the boys playing foul ball on local hospitality. It flustered him. "I don't understand—I'm afraid I don't understand, Mr. Harris."

"Who asked you to understand? Do I get the bodyguards."

He bowed, stiffly. "We try to make our guests feel at home, Mr. Harris. Is there any other way we can be of service to you?"

I took out my new bill-fold. It was fat with Colonel Wedgewood's money. Bug-eyed, the manager watched the wad of five-hundred-dollar bills I took out and leafed through.

"Let's see—seventeen thousand. Will you put this in the safe for me? Leave the receipt at the desk."

"Of course, of course—uh—seventeen thousand," he mumbled, counting the bills. "You don't wish to come down and sign for it, Mr. Harris?"

"If I did, I would," I gave him. "But I don't."

He nodded and left in a daze.

The scene had left Bitters breathing heavily through his nose again.

"Unpack!" I snarled at him. "Don't stand there looking as if you're in a psychopathic ward! I didn't hire you to look surprised at what I do."

"Indeed so, sir," Bitters answered hastily. "I understand you perfectly, sir. I mean-er—I'll try to understand you perfectly. Unpack, sir—that was what you wished, wasn't it?" Bitters babbled, looking like his dinner had come to life and snapped at him.

"It is," says I, turning to the bedroom. "Order Scotch and soda."

THE MANAGER MAY have left in a daze, but he gave service. By the time I was dressed for dinner, two big huskies were stationed outside my door. I stepped out, looked them over, and spoke to the one on my right, "What's your name?"

"Joe Jacobs," he rumbled, looking down his nose, past a face that would have made a mother weak. He had a cauliflower ear, a scar on his jaw, and the shoulders and neck of a wrestler.

"And you?" I asked the other man.

He looked down, too, blinked, and said, "Gus Wayland's me name, Boss. What're we supposed to do?" He had a flat nose, long arms, powerful hands and the trusting brown eyes of a good-natured spaniel.

"All you've got to do, Gus," I explained, "is keep close to me when I tell you to, and not let anyone touch me. You're bodyguards. Get it? Bodyguards."

"*Har*—it's a pipe!" Gus chortled, with a confidential wink.

"Take that smirk off your map!" I ordered. "D'you think you're starring in a two-ring circus?"

Gus straightened his face, snapped to attention—and when I went down to eat a few minutes later both of them trotted at my heels as solemn and formidable as two work elephants behind a fox terrier.

When we disgorged from the elevator into the lobby, two more huskies standing nearby took their cue and closed in also.

"Don't crowd so much or I'll suffocate!" I snarled from inside that towering wall of meat. "Deliver me to the dining room and wait at the door."

The dining room was crowded. My ten-dollar tips had been like a shot of yeast to the hotel staff. The headwaiter led the charge. A "reserved" sign was whisked off a table. Waiters flocked around. The head-waiter himself took my order. Diners turned in their chairs and stared at the show.

I looked around for Trixie Meehan—and spotted her at a table across the room.

Little Trixie was dressed in white. She looked fragile, lovely, and very, very helpless. But she had protection. He was past forty, rather sallow, but well-turned out, jaunty and good-looking in a dinner jacket.

I knew the type. He was a wise boy—New York wise—self-assured, smug. But Trixie had him hooked. He was watching her as if fearful the luscious little tidbit might flit away.

Trixie saw me and ignored me. She was working on

her escort as if she had suddenly discovered something devastating.

They left before I did. They were not in sight when I emerged from the dining room. So, with my squad of huskies I paraded the lobby, the patios and out on the ocean terrace for the benefit of the crowd.

They ate it up. I ignored them, and in half an hour went up to the suite and telephoned Trixie's room.

She was out then, and was still out next three times I called her. Hours later the telephone beside my bed rang. Trixie cooed over the wire.

"Apsay, do you think you're another Napoleon with that army of flat-feet?"

"Does this look like Moscow?" I snarled back. "Who was that jumble-brain you speared for the dinner check?"

"*And* the evening, Useless," says Trixie. "We're at the Club Monte now. He dances divinely—and his taxi technique is devastating. I didn't dream," Trixie sighed, "that the job would turn out as amusing as this."

"Get a load of cold turkey!" I snarled at her. "You aren't here to take up taxi wrestling! Ditch that shined-up Romeo and do something about the Palmer woman's lawyer! I *told* you what to do!"

"So thoughtful of you, too, Mike," Trixie cooed. "I've been with him all evening. As a wealthy young widow, I'm a riot. Louie's weakness is wealth *and* the widow's mite."

"So it's Louie already?"

Trixie giggled. "What a man he turned out to be, Mike. *What* a man!"

"Never mind his score card. Will he talk?"

"Louie," says Trixie cheerfully, "is a gentleman—except

in the clinches. Besides, he's smart. He asks questions, but he does hate to talk about his business. Give me time."

"You'll be dizzy by then, with a can tied to you. What about La Palmer?"

"Look for the prettiest one," Trixie said sweetly. "She's all of thirty-four—and admits to twenty-five, and gets away with it, if the beauty shop gossip is right. The cats usually are. Her hair is corn-colored and she's about your height, Mike. Tonight she was wearing white and gold—and Louie is in her bad graces because of poor little me. Isn't it thrilling?"

"Bring that powder-rubber home and knock off for the evening."

That got me a giggle. "I'm only starting—and I hope you don't like it," Trixie gave me. *"Au revoir,* Napoleon. Don't fall over your ego." She hung up on me.

That was Trixie—in my hair already. I bawled out Bitters, had a long Scotch and soda, with visions of Trixie cuddling for that shyster, and finally got to sleep.

In the morning when I crawled out of bed, Bitters handed me a note in a hotel envelope. "This was in your box, sir."

It was from Trixie, of course; three words: *She swims early.*

So I swam early, too.

3

BAIT

THE WHITE BEACH sand sloped from the hotel terrace to
the shallows where mile-long combers broke in creamy
smothers. Gay beach umbrellas dotted the sand. An early
crowd was out when I hit the ocean with my four husky
guards.

We drew a quick gallery. Celebrities were a dime a dozen
at the Miami-Plaza, but four ponderous bodyguards were
a show. The crowd had nothing to do but look and talk—
and they did.

On our second circuit of the beach I spotted the Palmer
woman under an umbrella. Bradley was right. What a
woman. In her scanty bathing suit she outclassed anything
on the beach. She was small, slender, perfect. Her face had a
sultry, vivid beauty that was worth money to any smart girl.

And down beside her on one knee, talking vehemently,
was Layre, the lawyer. He paid no attention to me as I
paraded by. But Lucille Palmer spared one flickering glance
of appraisal. Nothing personal. She probably estimated
every man.

By the time I turned back along the beach again, Layre
was walking away and Lucille Palmer was heading toward

the water, adjusting her green rubber cap. I dunked the body also.

The surf was brisk. She swam out and met the breakers shoulder high. I swam out beyond her at an angle, and drifted back in, laying a bearing on her green cap. In the white smother of a breaking wave I rolled in against her.

We both staggered, fighting for footing until the wave washed past. She was annoyed until she recognized me; and then her face changed.

"Excuse me," I gasped. "I'm not a very g-good swimmer!" And I grabbed her hand and balanced myself.

She let me hold on. "You're the man with the bodyguards," she said, studying my face while we both braced for the next wave.

"Yes, ma'am."

The wave hit us, threw us together, and when we were clear she asked, "Why do you need those four big bruisers to guard you? What are you—a—a what they call a big-shot?"

"Oh, dear me, mercy no!" I denied breathlessly. "My lawyers suggested the guards. Isn't this great? Look out— here comes the next wave!"

We went together again. When we came out of the smother, Lucille gave me a sidewise look.

"No," she said dryly, "you couldn't be."

"Couldn't be what, ma'am?"

"A big-shot," she said coldly, wading back to shallower water. "And I'll take my hand if you don't mind. Just what are you, Mr. Harris?"

"D-do you know my name?"

Her laugh was throaty. It matched her sultry looks, as

she said: "How could I help it? Everyone in the hotel is asking about you."

"Heavens!" I gulped. "I didn't mean to attract attention. I—I think I'd better wire my lawyers—er—Miss—"

That drew me another throaty laugh.

"I'm Lucille Palmer. You are a funny man. Tell me why your lawyers insist on those bodyguards?"

I sighed mournfully. "Too much money, I suppose. Kidnapers and all that sort of thing, you know. I've been miserable ever since I inherited the estate."

"Estate?"

"Cousin Jeffry's estate," I sighed. "His health was perfect, too. If the train had been only two minutes later that last time he got drunk—"

"Tch, tch—" Lucille said sympathetically. "So Cousin Jeffry was killed in a train wreck?"

"Not exactly. I don't think the train was wrecked. But if it had been a little late, Jeffry would have gotten over the grade crossing in time. He always was impetuous."

"Impetuous," said Lucille queerly. "It must have been a shock. And you're unsteady now from those waves, aren't you? Here, give me your hand. We'd better sit on the sand and rest a little."

So we sat on the sand—and I told Lucille about the Bon Ton glove counter where I used to work, and the trials of having so much money now.

Lucille patted my hand sympathetically. "You don't play enough, Michael. And if you wish, you may call me Lucille."

"Lucille," I sighed.

"Lawyers," Lucille murmured dreamily, "have to earn

their money by giving advice. But you don't have to be silly enough to take it, Michael."

"Would—would you take a drive with me, Lucille?"

"Of course I would, Michael. And we won't need any bodyguards, will we?"

"Well—"

"No bodyguards," said Lucille firmly. "I'm all the protection you need."

BITTERS WAS AT the telephone when I entered the suite. He hung up hastily. I thought he looked guilty. But his voice was as ugubrious as ever.

"Can I mix you a drink, sir?"

"Who were you telephoning?"

"I thought you might need another bottle of Scotch, sir. I took the liberty of ordering it sent up."

"Fair enough," I said. "Go down and get me the papers."

When Bitters was out of the way, I got the switchboard.

"This is 318," I said. "Mr. Harris talking. The telephone was used here a few minutes ago. Who was called?"

"Just a moment, Mr. Harris. Outside, I think— Yes, the Atlantic Hotel. Do you wish the number?"

"Who was being called at the Atlantic Hotel?"

"I can't tell you that, Mr. Harris."

"Never mind the number."

So Bitters had lied. Why? He'd been hired from a New York employment agency. References were in good order. He was the perfect gentleman's gentleman—just what I needed for this act. But now—what about Bitters?

When he returned with the papers, Bitters' long solemn face was slightly disapproving—no different than it had been since we had arrived.

"Will there be anything else, sir?"

"Not now," I said. "I'm going for a drive."

Lucille and I, minus the bodyguards, drove behind a chauffeur in a sixteen-cylinder job I had rented. We came back with a date for dinner.

That afternoon, three bellhops collected their twenty-dollar bills. People had been asking questions about me—a Mrs. Nicolby, the current gossip—Louis Layre, the lawyer—and Lucille Palmer's maid. A business woman was Lucille.

Bradley telephoned: "Colonel Wedgewood is demanding action, Mike. They're crowding him for the money. Any luck?"

"Tell him to stall them. Rome wasn't burned in a day."

"Rome," says Bradley, "never was burned up like Colonel Wedgewood is now over your expense account and the delay. For God's sake, Mike, give me some action for his money!"

"Give him sweet hope," I said. "And you haven't seen an expense account yet." I hung up before Bradley could erupt.

Lucille's black lace frock that evening infuriated every other woman in the dining room. So Lucille felt good. Afterwards we went to the dog races out north of Miami, taking two of my guards, at my insistence.

With palms and pines flanking the grandstand, and the dogs chasing the mechanical rabbit around the brightly lighted arena, while the crowd yelled and rooted, I bet hard and heavy. And lost one—two—three.

"You're reckless with your money," Lucille chided.

Bradley would have groaned at my reply. "It's nothing. I hardly know what to do with the stuff."

I'd told Gus and Joe, my guards, to keep their seats. Lucille and I were edging back to our seats in the grandstand before the fifth race. Lucille's arm, which I held, suddenly went tense. Her eyes, at the moment, were on the seats over to the left. Only one man was looking full at her.

A smooth smile of satisfaction was widening on his face. Smooth, florid, well-barbered, nattily dressed, he had the same wise look as Louis Layre.

The blonde who sat beside him looked like a Broadway chorus girl. And probably had been one.

Lucille Palmer was not smiling. Her makeup emphasized a sudden pallor. I watched her. The fifth race didn't mean anything to her.

I caught her digging fingernails into the palm of her hand. While the pooches were running, she watched that third row ahead, where the blonde and her escort were seated.

Once the man looked around at us. He'd noted where our seats were.

Rasputin, my hound, chased the rabbit in first for a change. The band began to play; the crowd surged from the seats again. Lucille moistened her lips.

"I—I've got to make a telephone call, Michael. Don't bother to come."

"It will be a pleasure," I gave her primly.

I thought she was going to refuse. "Come along, then," she said abruptly.

The closed door of the telephone booth cut off her

words. But through the glass she looked nervous, excited. As a matter of fact, she looked frightened.

"Lousy bunch of hounds here tonight."

He'd come down out of the grandstand without his blonde. He was smiling affably. "Cigarette?" he asked, opening a flat case.

I HAD TO think fast to remember the Bon Ton glove counter and Cousin Jeffry. "Why—why, do I know you, sir?"

"Huh—what's that?" He gave a quick, narrow-lidded look. "I get it," he said, half to himself. Then he chuckled. "I know your lady friend, so it's all right, friend. The name is Cushman. Bernard Cushman. What'd you say your name was?"

"Harris, sir. Mr. Michael Harris."

"Well, well—it's a pleasure, Mr. Harris. And here's the little lady herself."

The little lady was edging out of the telephone booth with her hand in her purse. If she didn't have her hand on a gun, I was nobody's business. All color had left her face. The rouge stood out. She was tense, like a cat coming out of a corner ready to fight.

Cushman ignored it with a bland smile. One hand out to shake hands, and the other holding the cigarette case, he said: "You're the last kid I was lookin' for down here. Lots of surprises, eh? Haven't changed your name, have you—gotten married, or anything like that?"

"I'm still Lucille Palmer, Bernie." She had a dangerous note of warning. I wondered what her name had been when they knew each other before.

Cushman chuckled.

"Never mind introducing me, Lucille. I've met Mr. Harris already."

"So I see." Lucille closed her purse with a snap. Her voice had a snap, too. Color was coming back into her cheeks. Her fear was giving away to suppressed fury.

Cushman ignored that, too. He had a bland, smooth manner. "Where you staying?" he questioned.

"Does it matter? I won't be seeing you while I'm here. I'm—busy."

Cushman chuckled again. "First time I've ever seen you too ritzy to pass up old friends. Say—I've got a sweet idea. You an' your friend join us. We're due at a live party in a while."

"No, *thanks!*"

Cushman urged: "You know the fellow—Jack Wetzlaff. He's got a yacht he won in a deal a few months ago. Just brought it down from New York, and he's throwing a party on board tonight."

"Steady, Mike," says I to myself.

I was suddenly all ears. Wetzlaff was in the New York rackets—high up. He'd made plenty; was still making it. The devil only knew what kind of a deal had given him a yacht. Some poor lad had been squeezed hard.

Lucille's anger abruptly vanished. "A yacht?"

"It'll knock your eyes out."

"I didn't know you were running around with Jack Wetzlaff."

"We're like that." Cushman crossed his fingers.

And I horned in. This was a chance to take. Crooks aren't smart. Pour a few drinks into one when he thinks the company is "right," and his tongue usually wags.

"A party on a yacht would be fun," says I, hesitatingly.

"I doubt it," Lucille came back positively. "I think you'd better take me back to the hotel, Michael. I'm getting a headache."

Cushman grinned. "Let's take Lucille back to her hotel, and then you come on to the party with us, Mr. Harris. There'll be an extra girl for you if you want one."

Lucille scorched him with a look. I visibly weakened. She forced a smile.

"If Michael goes, I'll take an aspirin and go, too. Someone might start a poker game. I don't think Michael's poker is good enough."

I felt like a tasty morsel of meat they were bristling over. It didn't matter. Maybe Lucille would talk, too, after a few drinks....

So we went to the party, taking my bodyguards.

4

A TOAST TO TREACHERY

THE YACHT WAS tied alongside the causeway, with the fairy-like blaze of lights along the Biscayne Boulevard waterfront gleaming across the water to the west. The fainter lights of Miami Beach showed at the other end of the causeway to the east.

Jack Wetzlaff's yacht had cost someone big money. Windows and portholes were gleaming with light when we went aboard. The party was already high.

I told my men to wait outside—and went in as nervous as a hen with pups. Someone on board might know me. The lid would come off then.

Five minutes later, no one in the mob cared whether I was Dinty Moore or the Emperor of Africa.

There was a good sprinkling of dinner jackets and evening gowns, including Lucille and myself. A smart dick from Centre Street probably could have identified sixty percent of them.

Wetzlaff looked better than his rogue's gallery photograph. He was a short, stocky man, with a blue-black jaw, a pointed nose, ears flat to his head, and patent-leather black hair parted smoothly at the side. A big diamond glinted on his right hand. His face was flushed and he was bawling the words to the song as he hauled a droopy-lidded brunette around in a bad tango.

They'd cleared the saloon floor and were dancing to phonograph music. White-coated stewards were rushing drinks. To give the devil his due, the girls were all lookers. The men were in the money. Your crook is a picker when his bankroll can stand the tariff.

Bernie Cushman's blonde—there was something familiar about Cushman—called herself Verna Shane. She was nice to me. Cushman's orders, I guess.

Wetzlaff spotted us, ditched his girl, came over to greet us. You could tell he and Cushman were thick. Lucille Palmer got the welcome of an old friend. She looked nervous, on edge. She introduced me reluctantly.

"Mr. Wetzlaff—Mr. Harris."

Cushman chuckled and said: "Jack is in Wall Street, Mr. Harris. You might remember him when you're investing money."

Wetzlaff had probably never gotten below Houston Street. He would have been pinched around Broad and Wall. I couldn't resist a crack as I took his moist hand, which, surprisingly, was powerful. I remembered then that Wetzlaff had once been a stevedore.

"I'll remember Mr. Wetzlaff when I need a broker. Everybody's going into Wall Street now, aren't they?" I cracked.

Wetzlaff gave me a quick look. Somebody must have given him the high sign. His face cleared into a welcome smile.

"I'll be on tap for your extra money, Mr. Harris. You won't even have to look me up. I'll get in touch with you."

They seemed to think that was funny—all but Lucille. She said, with a warning edge: "I'll let you know when Michael needs you."

Grinning, Wetzlaff said, "How about a drink?" He looked around, snapped his fingers. A white-coated steward swerved over to us with a tray of glasses—and we were launched in the party in a tide of liquor.

Wetzlaff took Lucille's arm and led her aside. Cushman left his blonde with me. She'd have nothing but a dance.

Maybe it was the liquor—maybe the memory of Trixie and Louis Layre that made me willing enough. But while we danced my mind was working.

Why, I asked myself, had Lucille been so upset when she saw Bernie Cushman? Whom had she telephoned so quickly? Layre, her lawyer? And why had she come out of that telephone booth with her hand in her purse, as if she were expecting a gun? And why, after hearing that Cushman was friends with Jack Wetzlaff, had her guard come down a little?

I couldn't spot a hook-up between all that and Colonel Wedgewood.

Bradley had said Lucille and her lawyer were in Miami Beach alone. They seemed to be putting the screws on Colonel Wedgewood by themselves, with only a two-way split to the money.

But you couldn't tell. Show me a smart woman of the underworld, and usually I'll show you a crook or two behind her. Sometimes more. The molls simply don't work much alone.

Vera was perspiring when we finished the dance. She wanted air. We went out on deck....

MY TWO HUSKIES were standing at the rail, puffing cigarettes. Near them a slim young man in a dinner jacket was
staring at the automobile headlights moving along the
causeway, between Miami and Miami Beach.

Gus Wayland, the big fellow with the flat nose, the long
arms, and the trusting brown eyes of a good-natured spaniel, touched my arm as I passed.

"Can you talk to me a minute, Boss?" he asked hoarsely.

"In just a moment."

The blonde giggled as I parked her at the rail. "Honestly,"
she said, "that army you drag around paralyzes me, Mr.
Harris. What good are they?"

"They're my bodyguard. Suppose someone tried to
kidnap me?"

She giggled again. "Get wise, Mike. Do you really think
those two gorillas would be any good if some smart boys
decided to take you?"

"Why—why, the agency guaranteed them, Miss Shane!"

She eyed me in the moonlight, and shook her head sadly.
"I wouldn't believe it if I didn't hear it right here," she
stated. "I didn't think there was one left."

"I—I don't understand, Miss Shane."

"You wouldn't." She became scornfully candid for a
moment. "Listen, they'd chase those gorillas up the first
alley so fast the hams wouldn't know what happened.
Somebody sold you a pair of cranberries. Why, that guy
there at the rail—" She broke off.

The young man she mentioned was ignoring us.

"Yes?" I prompted.

She shrugged. "Nothing. I'm gettin' gabby like I always
do when I hoist a few. Go on and talk with your nurse-

maid. He's got the fidgets. I guess he's gotta earn his money some way."

Big Gus led me down the deck out of earshot. He ducked his head, so his whisper reached my ear alone. "Lissen, Boss!" he husked. "It ain't none of my business. I'm gettin' my dough for taggin' you around an' takin' orders. But I don't like the looks of this gang you muscled into."

"I don't see anything wrong."

"That's what's worryin' Joe an' me. Joe says, 'I'll bet Mr. Harris ain't wise to these eggs. Maybe we better slip it to him straight.'"

"Go on," I said. "Tell me about it."

In the moonlight Gus looked at me doubtfully. "Sometimes," he sighed, "you sound all right, Boss. An' sometimes I ain't so sure. Anyway, if you need bodyguards, this ain't no place for you to be. Joe an' I been lookin' this crowd over. They're mugs."

"What makes you think they're bad for me?"

"Lissen, that guy back there at the rail is watchin' Joe an' me. He's packin' a rod under his arm. Maybe it's all right— but what's he watchin' us for?"

"Thanks," I said. "Keep your mouth buttoned and your eyes open."

My blonde was ready to go in. Lucille Palmer met us inside. "Thanks for giving so much attention to my friend," she said in a voice that would have cut metal.

The blonde smiled sweetly as she left. "Anything for *you*, dearie."

"That girl will make me mad some day," Lucille said ominously.

"She was nice to me," says I timidly.

"She would be," says Lucille through her teeth. "Here, have a drink."

A steward was there with two glasses on his tray. Lucille handed me one, took the other as if she needed it. "Here's to—us," she said, smiling over the rim.

I DRANK TO that. She was all I wanted—as long as she had Colonel Wedgewood's letters. And I wondered if she'd start talking after a few more drinks—

I was still wondering about it when I woke up, coughing and choking.

The biting fumes of ammonia were in my nose and throat. A light was glaring in my eyes. I was lying on a bed with my clothes on. The stocky figure of Jack Wetzlaff was bending over me, holding a handkerchief to my nostrils.

I pushed his hand away and sat up, gasping for breath. Cold, weak and sick, I saw at once I wasn't aboard the boat. The room was too big. It didn't look like a hotel room either.

"What's the idea?" I gasped, putting my feet over the edge of the bed and rubbing my bleary eyes.

Wetzlaff's smile was not too pleasant. "Got a head on you, hunh? No wonder, after all those drinks you put down. Your pulse was going ragged, so I thought we'd better wake you up. You can go back to sleep now."

I looked at my wrist watch. It was a quarter to four. "Where am I?" I groaned.

"In my house," Wetzlaff told me. "You're all right. Go on back to sleep."

But I persisted. "What am I doing in your house and where's Miss Palmer?"

"She went home."

"Where's my bodyguards?"

"They went home, too."

"Why didn't I go with them?"

Wetzlaff grinned—and it looked nasty.

"You stayed with the party. Nobody could stop you. I never seen anyone hoist the booze like you did."

I could remember that drink Lucille Palmer had handed me. After that there was some vague talk through the noise and music. I'd sat down, feeling sleepy—

But there'd been no wild drinking. I don't do it. Wetzlaff was lying.

One drink had done it. That meant knockout drops. Had Lucille done that?

Wetzlaff's mention of my weak pulse hinted at part of the truth. I'd been given too strong a dose. My condition had become alarming; he'd worked on me and brought me around.

I wasn't having any more sleep. Sick and weary as I was, and still dopey, I knew this was no place for Mike Harris. If I'd been given knockout drops, there was a reason.

"I think I'll go back to the hotel," I said, standing up giddily.

"It's too late," Wetzlaff said curtly. "Go on back to sleep. You're all right."

I started toward the door. "I'll go back to the hotel," I insisted. "Sorry to have bothered you this way."

I saw it coming—but I couldn't dodge. He hit me on the cheek and knocked me back across the bed.

"All right—you want it, an' you'll get it!" I heard him snarl as I bounced on the mattress. "An' for much more, I'll take a rod an' put the heat on you myself, you lousy dick!"

5

MOONLIGHT FLIGHT

WETZLAFF'S WORDS HIT me harder than his fist. I'd fumbled the job. They knew who I was. That explained the doped drink, the watch which had been put on my bodyguards.

I was almost sick enough to lie there and take it. But I was too mad. I'd spent Colonel Wedgewood's money like a drunken sailor. I'd put on an asinine act that had even made Trixie Meehan razz me. And all the while I'd only been making a fool out of myself.

Wetzlaff's lower lip was shoved out in a snarl as he bent over the bed. "Had enough, rat?" he grated. "Or do you have to get the works before you get the idea?"

I was on my side, half doubled up. My left leg was crooked. I kicked him in the stomach as he finished.

He doubled up with a loud grunt, and hurtled back across the room into the wall. When I came off the bed he was bent over, face livid, muscles paralyzed, breath gone for the moment.

I'd have tackled him—but I already knew how strong he was. His right hand was fumbling under his coat. The moment he caught his breath and got the gun, he'd have me.

I got through the doorway just in time. His gun roared behind me. I didn't look around to see where the bullet hit.

I seemed to be in an upstairs hall. Ahead was a flight of stairs going down. Further along the hall, Cushman's blonde was just stepping out of a doorway in a peach silk negligee.

She screamed as the gun went off; screamed again as I dove for the stairs…

The winding flight of steps was only a blur. So was the lighted hall below. Just before I reached the bottom, a man wearing a dinner jacket and holding a liquor glass in his left hand stepped out of a doorway at the right, directly into my path. Vaguely I remembered having seen him on the yacht—

That was all I remembered. He hurled the glass. It splattered the front of my coat—and I was on him an instant later.

His fist hit my shoulder. Then I smashed him on the jaw with my flying weight behind the blow. We crashed to the floor together and brought up with a slam against the front door.

He was out like a bundle of old clothes. My hand felt as if it were broken. In the next room women were crying out, men were shouting, as I staggered up and yanked on the door.

Wetzlaff's yell of warning came down the steps as I left the house. "*Stop him!*" Then I slammed the door behind me so hard the glass shattered.

I dashed over a flagstone terrace onto a smooth lawn. And there was the sea before me—placid and lovely beyond a beach of smooth, white sand.

A low, wooden pier ran out a hundred yards or so into the water. In the dying moonlight, it looked like a dark, spidery tentacle reaching out from shore.

Wetzlaff's yacht probably docked there, I thought, as I dashed across the lawn. Behind me lights went on at the front door. Loud, excited voices clamored on the night. Guns spat after me....

I HEARD THE strident whine of passing bullets. One bullet *plunked* audibly in the sod by my left foot. But the moon was almost down, the light was bad, and I was moving fast toward a fringe of palms and palmetto fringing the lawn and running along the beach.

Unharmed, I reached the black shadows under the first palms and cut along the beach to the right. They didn't seem to be following. It wouldn't have been much use anyway. The undergrowth gave too much cover.

One thing puzzled me. I didn't recognize the beach. It wasn't Miami Beach, or along the shores of Biscayne Bay. The surf had the slow, powerful surge of the open sea.

Wetzlaff's place, obviously, was somewhere along the coast north or south of Miami. There'd be another house somewhere ahead; a telephone, an automobile, perhaps, to get me back to the hotel.

And when I got there Lucille, the wench, was going to get shocked into her age—unless she'd lammed already.

Then I thought of Gus and Joe, my bodyguards. If I'd been doped, what of them? Wetzlaff and La Palmer must have known there'd be a kick-back from this. They couldn't take chances on those two men talking. By that time I was as cheerful as a flood of tears.

I stopped, listened, heard no sounds of pursuit. So on I

went. This stretch of coast was lonely. The dry sand whispered underfoot. The big palm leaves rustled dryly. The undergrowth at my right seemed to grow thicker, wilder.

The moon went down and the night was black. The breaking waves had little ghostly ripples of phosphorescence. Now and then the beach curved gently. No lights appeared.

I was still shaky, weak. My right hand was swollen and sore. The sand made walking hard. I began to tire, but I kept on stubbornly. When daylight came, I wanted to be a long way from Wetzlaff's house. For they'd come after me. They couldn't afford to let me get away. If I rested, went to sleep; if I slowed up and let them get in sight of me after daylight, it would be farewell, sweet farewell for Mike Harris. And I liked him in spite of his dumb mistakes.

So, dopey and half-asleep, I kept going. The palms were black and mysterious on my right, the sea shimmered vaguely on my left, the pale strip of white sand stretched out ahead, and I plodded on—on—on....

Wouldn't there ever be another house? Didn't anyone else live along this stretch of the coast? Then, suddenly, the palms ended—and there was a house with lighted windows, with rest and safety. Sweet safety. Sweet rest.

Mike Harris could still run. I discovered that as I crossed a lawn and came to the house. Just before I reached the door someone called over at my left: *"Stand still, damn you!"*

And the heartbreaking truth hit me like a blow. The door glass was broken. I had merely made the circuit of an island—and was back at Wetzlaff's house again. They had me, and I was helpless....

6

TRIXIE SHOWS

THEY CAME AT me from two sides, trapping me there by the door. Three of them. I thought they were going to shoot. Instead, for thirty seconds after they reached me, they hit me with everything but the flagstones underfoot.

Fight back? I tried. What chance did I have? They even kicked me after I went down.

From what they said as I was yanked up again, I gathered they had spotted me returning along the beach, had tumbled to what I had done, and had eased to the house and waited for me.

By that time, the front door was open, the lights were on, and Wetzlaff and his house guests were crowding out.

"Bring him in!" Wetzlaff snarled.

Hired eggs, tough eggs, had jumped me. Two of them held me by the arms and hustled me into a big, brightly-lighted living room. The first thing I saw was my bodyguards, Gus and Joe, sitting gingerly on the edge of straight-backed chairs. Their arms were tied behind, their ankles were loosely tied.

Gus Wayland turned one sorrowful brown eye toward me. The other was black-and-blue and swollen shut.

"Boss," Gus said reproachfully, "I seen it coming."

"But you didn't duck fast enough," Joe Jacobs grumbled sourly. He had the cauliflower ear, the scar on his jaw and the shoulders of a wrestler. And now, sour and morose, he scowled at me. "These guys say you're a detective," he said.

"Do they?" was all I could think to reply through my swollen lips.

A blue-black stubble covered Wetzlaff's face. He was chewing on the stub of a cigar. The big diamond on his right hand glinted as he took the cigar from his mouth and addressed me with savage sarcasm. "So you thought you'd lam out?"

"I wish I'd kicked you in the jaw before I left," I told him; and reached for a handkerchief to wipe blood from my lip. The mug on my right grabbed my arm. "You've already frisked me!" I snapped. "Don't be so nervous!"

"Shall I crack him, Chief?" he begged Wetzlaff.

"Not now. You've almost ruined him already."

The young man I'd met at the bottom of the steps had a strip of adhesive plaster on his cheek. His look was venomous.

And Bernie Cushman was grinning. Two other men, about his age, were strangers to me. I'd have picked them out at crooks in any crowd. Cushman's blonde was there, dressed again, and four other girls I remembered vaguely as having seen on the yacht. They were molls or they wouldn't be here. Everyone looked sleepy.

Wetzlaff chewed the stump of his cigar again and glowered at me. Then he rolled it over to the corner of his mouth and demanded: "What the hell were you doing with 'Dates' Palmer?"

"That her name?"

"Don't stall with me!"

"I met the lady at the Miami-Plaza. I never saw her before. She told me her name was Lucille Palmer."

"Yeah? What's *your* name?"

"Michael Harris."

"Where you from?"

"Cleveland," says I, with a faint glimmer of hope.

"What were you doing in Miami?"

Wetzlaff was talking as if, after all, he didn't know much about me. Had he been guessing upstairs? I hung on to the original story I'd given Lucille Palmer.

"I came to Miami to enjoy myself," I said.

"And hooked up with 'Dates' Palmer right off?"

"I met her while I was in swimming."

"What was the idea of the flash front and these mugs for bodyguards?"

"I've received kidnaping threats," I gave him with dignity. "My lawyers advised the bodyguards. Will you— you please explain all this?" I asked coldly. "The law, I assure you, will have something to say about it."

Wetzlaff chewed his cigar in silence.

Bernie Cushman shrugged.

"Well," he said, "there he is. What d'you make of him?"

Vera Shane, the blonde, spoke up petulantly. "I told you you were making a mistake, Jack."

Wetzlaff snatched a folded piece of paper from his pocket and shoved it out at me.

"If you're a young squirt on the loose, what the hell are you doing with this letterhead from the Blaine Agency in your billfold? What's this writing on the back?"

He almost caught me off-guard.

"Oh—that?" says I, thinking wildly. "Why—uh—while I was in New York, I hired detectives from the Blaine Agency. Those are some memoranda in my—uh—private shorthand. That top note says to write a letter to my Aunt Louisa, in Omaha, Nebraska. Her oldest son broke his ankle last month, and—"

"All right, dammit, all right!" Wetzlaff broke in angrily. He glowered at me. "But I don't like the way you went into action upstairs. You didn't act like no damn fool then."

"I—I was frightened, I'll have to admit," says I meekly.

The blonde hummed under her breath: *"What a hell of a mess—what a hell of a mess. When this red-headed lamb gets loose, then what, suckers?"*

Wetzlaff snapped: "Throw him in that attic room! Lock those other two mugs down in the old wine cellar! We've got to get some sleep!"

THE ATTIC ROOM was up under the eaves. A rabbit couldn't have crawled through its one small window. The air was hot, stale. An army cot comprised the furniture. The two men who had brought me up locked and bolted the door.

I went to sleep. There wasn't anything else to do.

The sun was glaring through the tiny window when a hand on my shoulder awakened me. One of the men who had brought me in was there by the cot.

"Wetzlaff says to get you washed up and bring you down for grub," he said curtly. "Make it snappy."

By the sun it was about noon. Out of that little hell-hole under the roof, with a quick shower, a shave with a safety razor he handed me, and in my clothes again, I felt better. A radio was playing downstairs. Dishes were clattering, people were talking, when my guard brought me into the dining room.

Wetzlaff set down a glass of beer and pointed to an empty chair on my side of the long table. "Get some groceries," he growled.

The men wore white linens and flannels. The girls were in gay sport clothes. Sleep had helped their dispositions. The guard stood behind my chair and I sat down gaping at Lucille Palmer, seated across from me.

She had blue shadows under her eyes. Overnight she had aged years. And she was in a vile temper.

"So you're here, too?" I queried.

"Oh, for God's sake! Do I have to listen to you gabble and bleat on top of everything else?"

"Dearie," said one of the girls silkily, "you liked it well enough last night."

Lucille snatched up her glass of beer. I thought she was going to hurl it at the speaker. Then she put it down and flared at Wetzlaff: "Tell those floozies to lay off me or I won't be responsible!"

"Let her alone!" Wetzlaff mumbled.

The rest of the meal was more amicable. Wetzlaff harked back to old times. I gathered Lucille had once worked the badger game and Wetzlaff had been one of the gang. He'd come a long way since then.

I gathered further that Lucille had turned a neat trick on Cushman two years before in San Francisco. Cushman had almost taken a rap because of it. He'd threatened to get her then. That explained why she had come out of the telephone booth looking for trouble.

When the meal was over, Wetzlaff spoke bluntly. "All

of you scram outside. I'm going to be busy for a little while." Then he directed my guard, "Take him in the living room. I want to talk to him in a few minutes."

In the living room I took a cigarette from a box on a table and smoked moodily. My guard loitered near the hall doorway. He had a gun in a pocket. I knew what to expect if I tried to make another break.

There was a library behind the living room. Wetzlaff was in there with Lucille Palmer. In the quiet which fell I could hear their voices. Wetzlaff's grew louder, threatening. Lucille came back at him angrily. I listened. And what did I hear?

Wetzlaff: "You've got those letters in Miami somewhere! Are you going to cough up?"

La Palmer: "For the tenth time, no!"

All ears by then, I heard Wetzlaff angrily say: "I've tried to give you the dope straight! With those letters and the squeeze I can give him, I'll make that two-timing old billy-goat cough up a half million! You've got no business monkeying with a set-up like that!"

Lucille snapped back: "Where do you get off telling me my business? Stick to your racket and I'll stick to mine! You've already spoiled one sweet sucker I was shaping up! There will be hell to pay over him!"

"Yeah?"

"Yeah!" said Lucille, hard and fighting mad.

Silence for a moment. Then Wetzlaff said something in a lower voice. Her reply was shot with sudden panic.

"So *that's* your out? All you guys in the racket are kill-crazy! You—you can't do anything like that!"

WETZLAFF LAUGHED AT her, ugly, sneering. After a

moment he asked, "Are you going to cough up those letters and take your split?"

"Louis Layre put you onto this, Jack! You're using the same arguments he gave me! The dirty, double-crossing rat!"

"Never mind Layre! Are you going to be reasonable?"

"No!" Lucille fairly screamed at him. "For the last time, *no!*"

Wetzlaff cursed her then. "We'll see about that!" And suddenly I felt sorry for Lucille Palmer.

Something else was on my mind at the same moment, too. A low, droning sound outside the house had swiftly increased in volume. I recognized it now as the motors of an airplane. They were sputtering, missing….

The front door opened. One of the men looked into the living room. "Where's Jack?" he asked the guard.

"Next room."

Wetzlaff opened the library door and met him.

"There's an amphibian plane landing here, Jack! Something's wrong with its motors!"

Wetzlaff began to swear again. His face was dark with anger. "We don't want anyone here!"

"Well, it's coming down!"

"I'll see about that!" Wetzlaff spoke over his shoulder to Lucille Palmer. "Wait in here with the boy friend until I get back." And to the guard, "Watch 'em both."

He hurried out with the other man.

I'd moved to the front window by then. Lucille joined me. The corners of her mouth were white, drawn. She was breathing hard from strong emotion.

She ignored me as we stared out the window at the

twin-motored amphibian plane which swooped low over the water beyond the pier. It landed amid sheets of spray and taxied with coughing, spitting motors to the beach.

Wetzlaff and his guests hurried down to meet it.

On its landing wheels, the amphibian wallowed slowly up on the smooth, dry sand. The engines stopped. Wetzlaff stepped forward and talked to the pilot.

He broke off as a young woman in a gay sport suit emerged from the plane, ducked under the wing and joined him. The pilot followed her. A few moments later Wetzlaff and the strange young woman started toward the house. She was laughing as they talked. And Wetzlaff was smiling broadly.

A sick feeling suddenly hit the pit of my stomach. That tiny, slender, good-looking little bundle of fluff strolling at Wetzlaff's side was Trixie Meehan!

7

A CHANCE TO DIE

LUCILLE PALMER RECOGNIZED Trixie also. I saw her startled expression, saw her bite down on her lower lip. Her eyes flashed to my face. Her expression wasn't pleasant.

Under her breath she said, "So she's here, too!"

Trixie's face was clear as she came to the flagstone terrace with Wetzlaff. Not a line of worry in it. She's never looked more cuddly and helpless, more lovely and happy. Just a lost little girl trustfully meeting the world. The windows were open. I heard her chuckle delightedly.

"Such a *lovely* house, Mr. Gadsden. How nice of you to have it right here where our plane broke down."

Wetzlaff's smirk was almost fatuous. The lug! "For a little lady like you, I'd have a house anywhere I thought she'd drop down. Here, sit under the umbrella at this table. I'll order something cold."

"So thoughtful of you," Trixie cooed.

Wetzlaff called an order in the front door and rejoined her. I heard Trixie telling him how she'd hired the plane for a joy-ride out beyond the Gulf Stream. After they finished the drinks, Wetzlaff stood up and said he'd show her the house.

The guard had closed the door between our room and

the hall. Lucille jumped up, walked to the door and called through. "Jack, I want to talk to you a minute!"

Wetzlaff came in alone. Lucille led him to the other end of the room, talked under her breath. I heard Louis Layre's name mentioned. Wetzlaff's face hardened. He nodded and rejoined Trixie in the hall.

Lucille lighted a cigarette and began to hum cheerfully under her breath. I felt like throttling her. She'd knifed Trixie in some way. And if Wetzlaff caught Trixie off-base just once....

I was afraid—horribly afraid.

Trixie saw most of the house but the living room. Outside again with Wetzlaff, I saw her staring at the plane. "Someone's helping my pilot," she said.

"One of my men," Wetzlaff said calmly. "He's an expert mechanic; he will find the trouble in no time."

"That's—comforting," Trixie said. Some of her gayety had vanished.

Wetzlaff lighted a cigar, leaned back in his chair and watched the two men working on the plane. He seemed to be waiting for something.

The two men at the plane suddenly started toward the house, one walking ahead of the other. Doubt turned to certainty; then fear swamped me as I made out Trixie's pilot being herded to the house with a gun in his back.

The pilot was pale, flustered, when he reached the terrace. "What's the idea of this gun?" he demanded of Wetzlaff.

The gunner, a long, rangy fellow in dirty white canvas trousers, replied for him. "Chief, he was pullin' a fast one. Nothin' wrong with those motors."

"Yeah?" said Wetzlaff. He was on his feet by then. So was Trixie.

The pilot was a good-looking young fellow. He shrugged. "If they're okay now, we'll take off and call it a day."

"Will you?" said Wetzlaff. "Rough him, Pete."

Callously the gun barrel beat the young pilot to his knees. Blood was trickling out of the poor devil's hair when he reeled to his feet, eyes staring, mouth working.

"Th-this has gone far enough!" he gasped. "She—she said it was a joke she was playing when she asked me to find this island and stall the motors and land. But I've had enough!"

At my right shoulder Lucille Palmer laughed nastily. "I knew there was something screwy when that hussy showed up. It's some more of Louis Layre's dirty tricks."

"Get away from me before I forget myself!" I snarled.

Only the guard's drawn automatic kept me from going out that screened window. For Trixie had snapped open her purse and was drawing a gun as she darted back from Wetzlaff's sudden grab.

I groaned as she stumbled over the chair behind her and Wetzlaff caught her arm. Little Trixie didn't have a chance after that. Wetzlaff twisted her arm and forced her to her knees. He tore the gun out of her hand and jerked her to her feet.

"So you're a tough little tart, after all!"

While I clenched my fists and stood taut and trembling, Wetzlaff questioned Trixie, twisting her arm until she moaned. He seemed to have an idea she was hooked up with Louis Layre, the lawyer. He might be doing business with the man, but he obviously didn't trust him.

Trixie gave him no satisfaction. More than a bullying racketeer was needed to break that gallant little kid's spirit.

Wetzlaff finally exploded in rage, "Lock this guy upstairs with that other fellow! This business is spouting enough screwy angles to give a man the d.t.'s!"

SO THE GOOD-LOOKING young pilot and I landed back up under the eaves. We looked at one another after the door was locked. He was still shaking. He moistened his lips.

"What the hell does this mean?" he groaned.

"What you don't know won't hurt you," I said. "Sit down and stop shaking. You're not dead yet."

"Dead?"

"It's a gag," I said wearily. "What is your name?"

"Jerry Thompson."

"Where are we?"

He stared at me. "Don't you know?"

"Would I ask?"

He sighed. "We're on one of the little islands out beyond the Gulf Stream. About eighty miles from Miami. Last Man Cay it's called. We're off the steam tracks and the air lines to Nassau. Stray conch fishermen are about all that ever drop by. Rich guys have built on some of these isolated cays in the last ten years. Less than an hour from Miami by plane," he said bitterly, "and we might as well be off the edge of the earth."

"We're still hanging on," I said. "Right now there's nothing to do but wait and see what breaks."

I didn't tell him as I tried the door that my heart was almost breaking over what might be happening to Trixie.

The door was solid, hopeless. Any attempt to break it down would alarm the house.

The hot afternoon hours dragged by. Suddenly we both rushed to the little window. The amphibian motors had begun to roar.

Through the tiny window we could see the propellers swirling sand off the beach. The amphibian trundled around, took the water, and as the motors died, it floated toward the pier. Two men made the bow fast to the pier with a line and came ashore.

"I wonder what they're going to do," Jerry Thompson said huskily.

"Probably sink it."

He swallowed. "I'm sunk myself then. I've been supporting a wife and two kids with that crate this winter."

An hour later there was activity in the house. Wetzlaff's yacht showed off the end of the pier. A speedboat raced ashore. Wetzlaff and his house guests went down to meet it, carrying suitcases. Lucille Palmer was with them. She didn't seem to be a prisoner.

"Taking her cut and liking it after all," I muttered.

"What's that?" Thompson asked.

"Never mind. But it isn't good news for us."

He groaned. "My wife will be worried. She'll think something's happened to me."

"Too bad," I said. Why tell him his wife was practically a widow already?

Evening came. Darkness fell. No water. No food. I said suddenly, "Are you game to take a chance?"

8

―

PAYOFF PARTNERS

THOMPSON LOOKED AT me doubtfully. "What kind of a chance?"

"To get out of here. You'll risk a bellyful of lead. But it's probably your only chance to see the family again. Think fast, brother, think fast."

I liked him for his answer. "What do we do?" he asked quietly.

I was already tipping the cot up. As quickly as possible I wrenched a leg off. "Got a knife?" I asked.

Surprisingly, he had. I sharpened the end of the leg. "Grab a sheet and catch," I said.

With the sharpened stick, I attacked the plaster, waist high on the sloping roof, which formed one side of the room. Thompson caught the fragments in the sheet before they rattled on the floor.

It was a screwy idea. But anything was better than waiting for Wetzlaff to get rid of us. Beyond the plaster there were lathes, held by light nails. Carefully I pulled them off and got access to the under side of the roof. One strip of board had to be cut through in two places with the knife. Then shingles removed. The cool night air which rushed in was a Godsend to our sweat-covered bodies.

I crawled out first and perched on the slant of the roof. Thompson followed. The moon was up. The ground looked a long way below.

Thompson whispered, "How do we get down?"

"We don't," I said. "We go inside. That girl's in there. And a couple more mugs we've got to take along. And don't tell me it's dangerous and you've had enough or I'll shove you off the roof right here."

"If I do, you can shove," he replied. I loved that Jerry Thompson like a brother from then on.

We crawled over the ticklish slant of the roof until we were above a side-porch roof. Hanging onto Thompson's wrists, I lowered myself. He gasped. He was slipping. I let go and dropped the last two feet. He caught himself, came sliding feet first over the edge a moment later, and I eased him to a footing.

We unscreened a darkened window and slipped into a bedroom.

Gus and Joe were probably still down in the old wine cellar. But where was Trixie? I could hear people shooting craps downstairs. A man swore disgustedly.

"That cleans me!" he exclaimed. "But for ten bucks I'll tow that bunch out in the plane an' sink 'em for you, Buck. I know you've got a weak belly."

A leer was in Buck's reply. "Yeah? And what about the dame?"

Silence down there. I could almost see them looking at one another. Another voice said, "All Wetzlaff said was he didn't want to see her again."

I was sick inside by then, and raging. Those swine mouthing over Trixie's lovely helplessness. To Jerry Thompson I whispered:

"How long will it take you to get out to that plane and start those motors?"

"I ought to do it in ten minutes."

I whispered an idea in his ear.

"Okay," he said under his breath, and slipped back out the window.

And I raised a leg of the bed, removed a castor, and tied it in the end of a pillow case. The result was comforting.

They were still rolling dice downstairs when I tiptoed along the hall and up to the attic floor again. The short hall up there had several more rooms along it. A small electric bulb gave dim light. Without much hope I tapped on the doors. Trixie Meehan's voice said, "Yes?" inside the second door.

"It's Mike."

"Wh-what are you doing out there, Mike?"

"Wait and see."

I unscrewed the light bulb. In the darkness I hammered on her door. Half a minute of that brought steps hurrying up from below. Were they all coming? No; it sounded like one man.

I crouched at the top of the steps and waited. He came tramping up grumbling, "What the hell happened to that light?" Then, louder: "What's the matter up here?"

I SWUNG THE pillow case. He pitched forward with a queer, gurgling sound. I broke his fall just enough to avoid jarring the house. When I turned on the light I saw he was the same ill-natured fellow who'd kept a gun on me earlier in the day. He'd left his gun downstairs. But he had the keys I wanted. A moment later Trixie was with me, whispering shakily:

"Mike, you darling! I knew you'd do something if you could! Where's Wetzlaff? Where's the pilot of my plane?"

"Wetzlaff's gone back to Miami with the Palmer woman. Your pilot's outside. How'd you happen to come here?"

"Your man told me over the telephone this morning that you'd gone to Havana with friends. It didn't make sense. You'd have told me. I met Louis Layre in the lobby. He looked nervous, and said he was in a hurry and would see me in half an hour. I followed him in a taxi. He went on board a yacht moored by the causeway. He wasn't there long. When he left I turned sightseeing tourist and talked to a sailor guarding the foot of the gangplank.

"He wouldn't let me aboard, but he was willing to kill the time talking. He looked sleepy, and told me the yacht had just come in from an all night trip. I couldn't get any more out of him. But from a sailor on the yacht tied up just ahead of that one, I found out the boat belonged to a Mr. Wetzlaff, who had a house on Last Man's Cay.

"Wetzlaff's name was all I needed. Louis Layre worried—the Palmer woman not around—you gone— Layre going aboard Wetzlaff's boat which had been out all night—and Wetzlaff owning an island off-shore, I hired that plane and flew out here to see if there were any trace of you."

"Well, you saw."

Trixie shivered in the crook of my arm. "I balled everything up, didn't I, Mike?"

"Sweetness," I said, "you forced Lucille Palmer's hand. Wetzlaff was trying to chisel in on the Wedgewood deal.

Louis Layre had sold out to him. Lucille wasn't having any of it. Now she's given in. They're going ashore to crack Wedgewood. The price is now up to half a million. And," says I, "Wedgewood will probably pay if they aren't stopped."

A yell came up from below. "What's keeping you so long up there, Buck? You fooling with that girl?" When Buck didn't reply, we heard them coming up.

I started sweating. Without a gun we were sunk. I thought of going through my room and out on the roof. But there wasn't time.

I'd been listening for the amphibian motors to start. Had something happened to Jerry Thompson? Wouldn't that motor *ever* start?

They were in the second floor hall now, two or three of them, coming fast.

"Get back in your room," I said thickly.

"We're not going to make it, are we?" Trixie said unsteadily.

"Not now, I guess. This is the payoff."

"Then I'll take it with you, Mike."

"Trixie—you're—you're pretty swell!"

"Yes, Mike?" Trixie said with a catch in her voice.

It was almost love—and just then, outside in the night, the amphibian motors racketed out into full-throated thunder....

9

BITTERS

WELL, WE DIDN'T have love. One of the men below yelled, "It's the plane, boys! Somebody's out there!"

They bolted back downstairs. We had the house to ourselves. I grabbed Trixie's arm and hustled her down so fast her teeth rattled.

When I got her out the back door with directions, I looked for the old wine cellar down in the basement. It wasn't hard to find. One of my keys unlocked the massive door. Dirty, unshaven, haggard, Gus lumbered out croaking:

"What's the score, Boss? Don't tell me they're letting us go!"

"I should tell you anything!" I cracked back. "Just keep coming!"

When we reached the kitchen, I heard a bewildered voice calling in the front hall. "Buck! Pete! Where the hell are you guys?"

My victim had gotten downstairs by himself. We heard him go out the front door, still calling.

I grabbed a newspaper off a chair as we started out the back. Then, on the back porch, I spotted a five-gallon oil can.

"Just what I need to put the frosting on the cake," says I aloud. I took the can back in, unscrewed the cap, slopped some of the contents out, then backed through the doorway and tossed a lighted match.

It was gasoline. The puffing explosion almost blew me out the back porch door.

Gus Wayland gulped: "What the hell you doing, Boss?"

"Disinfecting a rat's nest," I said. "Follow me if you want breakfast in the morning!"

The amphibian motors were roaring just off-shore. The big plane was wallowing parallel to the beach in the opposite direction from which I ran.

The ripping tear of sub-machine gun fire spatted against the sound of the motors. Wetzlaff's men were shooting from the beach as they kept abreast of the slowly moving plane.

Trixie was waiting under the palms where I'd told her to go.

"The plane's going the other way!" she protested as I caught her arm and urged her along.

"Don't argue! Come on!"

"Do you know what you're doing?" Trixie panted indignantly as I half-dragged her along.

"Stop talking, you little nitwit, and run!" I yelled, shaking her arm.

"Nitwit?" Trixie blazed. "Trying to be a caveman again, Ape?"

So we were at it again, fighting as we ran. Where was love now? Bah!

I ran them a quarter of a mile down the beach. By that time the amphibian had circled out from shore and was heading back toward us. I lighted the newspaper, waved the flaming torch. The motors revved up and the plane came racing over the water toward us.

"You knew it was going to pick us up all the time!" Trixie accused.

"If you had any sense you'd have known he was decoying Wetzlaff's men down the other way!" I snapped. I was still jumpy. Suppose Jerry Thompson struck a floating log? Suppose something went wrong at the last minute?

Thompson brought the plane in almost to the beach. We waded out. He helped us aboard. His left arm was wet with blood. "They hit you," I said.

He grinned. "Nipped me in the arm. It's cheap enough for the ticket out of here. Hang on. We're going places."

Windows and walls of the cabin were dotted with bullet holes. That close they'd come to Thompson and the gas tanks. The next moment the up-surge of the plane thrust me down in the seat as Thompson hunted the sky with motors gunned wide open.

Last Man Cay, so formidable, so threatening and menacing, was suddenly only an insignificant patch of land on a limitless, moon-dusted sea. Far below red flames were licking out of a toy-like house.

I had no regrets for that fire. But as we droned through the night sky and the slow minutes dragged, I wondered feverishly whether I had a chance now to keep my promise and break the Wedgewood case in time.

Jerry Thompson was still chipper when he brought us down in a long glide toward the seaplane landing fronting Biscayne Boulevard. He taxied up on the wooden apron and stepped back to us, grinning.

"Now," he said, "for the cops!"

"Great boy, keed!" I said. "But no cops right now. I've got to have a little free time."

"Hey?" says Jerry, squinting at me. "How come?"

"You made a thousand bucks today," I told him. "And repairs on your plane extra."

"Nix. I ain't asking for an extra cut. I got back, didn't I?"

"It's on the expense account," I explained. "The guy who pays will like it or else. But I need time, Jerry. I'm a private dick on a delicate case. You will earn that grand if you help me."

Jerry's face cleared. "Why didn't you say so? I'll get my arm fixed up and report to the missus."

"I'm staying at the Miami-Plaza," I said as I started for the door. "Michael Harris is the name. I'll be seeing you."

We got a taxi on Biscayne Boulevard and drove over the south causeway. Wetzlaff's yacht was not there. That wasn't any help.

PEOPLE STARED AT us as we entered the Miami-Plaza. We looked bad. The desk said Lucille Palmer had checked out. My mind was on Bitters as the elevator went up. Would Bitters be here? He was.

I entered so swiftly I caught him coming off my bed with a newspaper in one hand and a glass of my Scotch and soda in the other. His jaw dropped. His eyes bulged. He gasped:

"Why, sir, why—"

"Exactly!" I yelped. "Why, and *why the hell?* Put down that glass, you big tramp!"

His hand was shaking as he obeyed. "You look rather upset, sir," he gulped. "Uh—has anything happened?"

I stood on my toes and slammed an uppercut under his

jaw. He went back on the bed. Rubbing my knuckles, I let him have it cold turkey.

"So I went to Havana, did I? Come through with it, you pile of cheese! What do you know about it?"

"I—I don't understand, sir."

"Maybe this'll help you!" I raged, and mashed his nose with the next one.

He was moaning and holding a handkerchief to his bleeding nose when he wallowed up on the bed again. Big Gus Wayland spoke admiringly from the doorway.

"Attaboy, Boss! What a punch! How about lettin' me have him? I gotta crack someone before I feel right again."

"I'll give him to you in a minute if he won't talk."

"This is a case for the police!" Bitters moaned.

"Cops, huh? Well, I'm a copper myself! Who's your friend at the Atlantic Hotel?"

"D-do you know about that?"

"What d'you think?"

"Oh, my soul!" Bitters exclaimed wildly. "What will happen to my references? Let me explain, sir. It's this way, sir. Indeed it is, sir. I didn't know you were a detective. And I happened to mention to a friend I met that you were wealthy. One thing led to another. He asked me questions—"

"What's his name?"

"A Mr. Cushman, sir."

"So that's the nigger in the weeds, eh? You've been fingering wealthy suckers for Bernie Cushman and getting a split afterwards?"

Bitters' silence verified it.

"Where's Cushman now?"

Bitters said nervously: "He—he telephoned about two hours ago and said you wouldn't be back for several days. I—I was to wait here for further word."

I grabbed the telephone and called the Atlantic Hotel. Cushman had checked out. Next I telephoned our branch office. Bradley answered. When he recognized my voice, he yelled:

"So you're finally back? And if you give me a wise-cracking excuse, I won't be responsible! Where have you been? Where is Miss Meehan?"

"Calm down," I suggested.

"Calm down?" Bradley bellowed. "I am calm! What have you been doing? Blowing yourself to a good time, I suppose, on that expense money I was fool enough to give you! Do you know what's happened in the meantime?"

"You tell me," I said.

"Colonel Wedgewood," Bradley roared, "called me about two hours ago and fired the Blaine Agency off the case! He says you've bungled everything! He demands an immediate accounting of the expense money! He swore he'd get my job and yours!"

"I can explain—"

"Explain?" Bradley yelled. "Can you explain me back into my job? Can you explain why this case has suddenly gone to pieces in our hands? You know the Blaine Agency policy! Results and no excuses! All you need to explain now is that expense account you blackjacked out of me! And you'd damned well better account for every penny that's been spent!" Bradley warned ominously. He slammed up the receiver.

10

DOUBLING FOR TROUBLE

SWEET WELCOME HOME! Bradley's job gone—my job and Trixie Meehan's job probably gone—and an expense account that never could be explained, now that I'd failed. And Colonel Wedgewood due to be nicked for his half million after all....

I called Trixie's room. "Be ready to leave in ten minutes," I told her.

"Who gave you a whip? Simon Legree?"

"This is business and never mind the wisecracks!" I yelped.

"If I minded you," says Trixie, "I'd have been plucking at a straitjacket long ago. What's behind this sudden itch?"

"The sky's just fallen in on our heads! We're going to Palm Beach!"

Trixie, in a pinch, was a trouper. "I'll be ready," she promised instantly.

Joe Jacobs rubbed the livid scar on his jaw. "Palm Beach, hey? We goin' too?"

"You are! Bitters, if we're both not ready in ten minutes, Heaven help you! Joe, tell the desk to get a big car for me to drive to Palm Beach."

I was tying my necktie as I made for the elevator. Bitters

hurried between Gus and Joe like a prisoner heading for the guillotine. A minute after we hit the lobby, Trixie joined us.

The car was waiting. Trixie rode beside me, the others in the back. While we raced northward, I told Trixie of my talk with Bradley. She was floored.

"Mike, what can we do now? Colonel Wedgewood may have paid his money by now. They've had time to get to him."

"We'll soon see!" I said savagely, and sent the speedometer crawling higher.

It was after ten-thirty when we rolled across the Lake Worth bridge into Palm Beach. It took me another quarter of an hour to locate and reach the Italian-style villa of Colonel Wedgewood. The house and the high-fenced tropical garden at one side were a riot of light, color and sound. An Oriental garden party was in progress. They were dancing on a temporary floor out in the scented, swanky garden.

"*This* looks like Wedgewood is worried," I remarked disgustedly.

Trixie said, "You can lay this on his wife. Going in?"

"Come along," says I. "Gus, you and Joe watch that rat."

A doorman in baggy trousers, silk jacket and turban out of the Arabian Nights answered my ring. He looked down his nose at us. "Only guests in costume are admitted tonight, sir."

"Tell Colonel Wedgewood I want to see him on important business."

"Your name, sir?"

"Never mind my name."

His eyebrows lifted in understanding. "This way, please."

He led us to the right, along a narrow, tiled hall, and left us in a tiny corner room which was dim and quiet.

"Well," says Trixie. "That was easy."

"Too easy," I said. "I don't like the looks of it."

Some minutes later the door opened and the Sultan Shahriyar himself slipped into the room and closed the door. He was about my size. His gorgeous costume and turban flamed with phony jewels. A black, curly beard covered his face. He carried a package under his arm. And his beard was phony, too.

"Did you bring them?" he demanded in a rasping, querulous voice.

"Bring what?"

"Those letters. Who is this young woman?"

I almost yelled with relief. He thought we represented Wetzlaff or La Palmer.

"Have you got the money in that package?" I asked.

"There is two hundred thousand in bills and a certified check for the rest," he said waspishly. "I had the bank manager go down and certify the check. Where—where are the letters?" He was frantic with anxiety.

I sneered, "No backbone left, eh? We're the detectives who've been working on your case. Hide that money. We'll get your letters back. D'you mean to tell me they've got nerve enough to come here and collect?"

He reacted in a frenzy of rage.

"Yes, you fool! I'm paying to protect myself! I was promised results and all I got was excuses! Tonight I was called to the telephone by a strange man and informed the time was up, and it was going to cost me half a million now for delaying! Your useless delays cost me that much extra! Get out of here before I have you thrown out!" He turned to the door to make good the threat.

"It's sink or swim now," says I to Trixie. "Here we go off the end of the dock!"

MY ARM WAS around Colonel Wedgewood's neck as I finished. I yanked the spluttering old idiot back on the floor and stopped his mouth by shoving his turban down over his face.

"Hey!" says Trixie. "It's all off now!"

"It's all coming off," I panted. "Look the other way if you're embarrassed."

Five minutes later I was wearing Colonel Wedgewood's costume, including the false beard. The colonel was gagged, tied hand and foot with a light cord and parked behind the sofa.

"I suppose we needed something like this to polish off the day," Trixie said faintly. "Do they hang people here in Florida?"

"Why bring that up?" I said. "It will come soon enough. Keep an eye on that old Romeo and his half million. I'm going hunting."

"For what?"

"That's the hell of it," I confessed. "I don't know. You might try prayer while I'm gone."

The doorman spoke to me deferentially. "Will the gentleman and lady be leaving, sir?"

I shook my head and walked back to the garden party. I felt as insane as this play I was making. What chance did Trixie and I have with the Blaine Agency now?

But this much I knew. Wetzlaff was striking hard and quick for the money. He was sending someone here for it tonight. The doorman evidently had his instructions. Colonel Wedgewood would be notified. That meant me now. They'd bring the letters, of course. And I now had a gun under my left arm.

Meanwhile—what a party!

The tropical garden was hung with colored lanterns. Sultan Shahriyar's court had come to life and was dancing under the moon and stars.

A gay young slave girl in pearls, gauze and little else but a mask tapped me on the arm and quirked luscious lips.

"Aren't you dancing at all tonight, Colonel Wedgewood?"

They say the flesh is weak. How true!

"Colonel Wedgewood!" my partner reproved with a giggle, after we had made half a round of the floor. "I didn't know you were so—so *impetuous!*"

"*Ah-h-h!*" I sighed, and risked being a little more impetuous.

A moment later she said warningly, "*Oh-h-h—!*"

A hand caught my shoulder. A strong hand. A formidable hand. And a man-sized voice said icily, "*Eustace,* have you lost your mind?"

11

THE CREDIT AND THE CASH

IT WAS THE Sultana Scheherazade—veiled, jeweled, bangled and authoritative. No doubt about the authority. She outweighed two of my little slave girl. She was broad in the beam and giving off sparks as she took me off that dance floor like a snowplow going through a drift.

"Eustace, you're a fool! An outrageous, scandalous old fool! Haven't you any respect for me, capering around with that brazen young thing like an old billy-goat! I've a good mind to lock you in your room!"

Through her veil I could see a noticeable mustache over a hard, mean mouth. I forgave that wizened, trussed-up old fossil right there. A woman like this would drive any man to flesh and zip.

The dim light saved my disguise. "Bah!" I growled in my throat and stalked away before she could get set for another wave of abuse.

Not until then did I discover I was sweating again. That had been a close shave. But it was nothing to the shock I got not two minutes later.

An arm slipped through mine out under the palms. A smooth voice said sarcastically, "Has my sweet old daddy got the money ready?"

You're right. It was Lucille Palmer, costumed and veiled also. *"Ah—ah—gggg!"* I gulped in my throat.

She warned me with an edge to her voice, "I haven't got the letters on me, so don't try to pull any fancy tricks!"

"Where are they?" I said, rasping and querulous.

"Give me the money and the certified check and you'll get the letters immediately."

"This way."

"Your voice sounds queer. This isn't too much of a shock to you, is it, Daddy?"

"Grnthh…"

"Love," Lucille informed me cheerfully, "comes high. But you had your money's worth, didn't you, Daddy? And you won't need that money much longer anyway."

The nerve of her. I almost forgot I wasn't Colonel Wedgewood and bit back a blistering retort just in time. All the while I was wondering where the devil she had those letters.

"How'd you get in here?" I growled.

She chuckled.

"After I decided to attend your garden party I just had time to get a costume in Miami. I'd have been here sooner but the costumer delayed me."

The doorman had left his post. I stopped her in the hall near the room where Trixie waited, and went in alone. Trixie was gone. Colonel Wedgewood was still behind the couch out of sight. The packet of money was lying on the couch.

I beckoned Lucille in and handed her the package in silence.

She broke the string, opened the paper, looked at the

bundles of large-denomination bills and the certified check on top.

"You just couldn't take it, could you, Daddy?" she said sarcastically. "Well, thanks for the sentiment. I'll send flowers when your arteries give way."

"The letters!" I reminded her as she opened the door with that half-million cuddled in her arms.

"They're coming!"

A man in costume, turban and mask shouldered into the room. A second one stopped me in the doorway.

"You got it?" the first one demanded.

He was Wetzlaff. His companion was Bernie Cushman. Lucille Palmer said sharply, "It's all here. Give the old fool his letters and let's scram out of here."

Wetzlaff laughed unpleasantly.

"Give 'em up until that certified check's been cashed? Hell, no! He'll get 'em later on—if he toes the line to suit me!"

That was the gag I'd been looking for all along. Why should they give up the letters if they had a chance to hang onto them for a further club? But at least I now knew where they were. Wetzlaff had them.

He was the nearest to me. La Palmer was beyond him. Bernie Cushman was in the doorway. Wetzlaff was sneering as he turned away—and I slugged him right on the button. He went down cold and I grabbed for my gun.

"*It's a plant!*" Lucille squawked. "Lam for the car, Bernie!" She slammed the door as she went out, and Cushman faded with her.

I stayed with Wetzlaff. The letters were more important at the moment. It took me half a minute to locate them and get the packet out from under his costume. And his gun. He wore a business suit underneath, ready for a quick getaway.

"I've got your letters, Grandpop!" I called to the figure behind the sofa. "Now I'll try to get your money!"

BUT I KNEW the money was gone. They had a start on me. Their getaway was planned. Bernie Cushman had had time to collect his wits and go for a gun.

The front door was ajar. They'd gone out that way. I followed—and ran smack into a fight out in the street. An automobile was half pulled out from the curb, its motor running. Trixie had Lucille Palmer in the gutter, helpless with a jujutsu armhold. The bundles of bills were around their feet. Gus and Joe were just subduing Bernie Cushman and the driver of the car.

"She almost bumped me as she ran out!" Trixie gasped. "I recognized her and got your men to stop them!"

Gus Wayland knocked Bernie Cushman cold and turned to me uncertainly. "Holy cow, Boss! What happened to you?"

"Never mind!" I panted, grabbing up the bundles of bills and re-wrapping them in the paper. "Hold everything here! I'll be back in a minute!" Chauffeurs from the other cars were gathering around as I started back toward the house. "It's a joke," I called to them. "Don't get excited."

They probably didn't believe me. It didn't matter at the moment. I found Wetzlaff groggily crawling to his feet and feeling for his gun. I held a gun on him while I untied Colonel Wedgewood.

"Here's your letters," I said, cramming them into his

hand. "And there's your money. Do you want me to call the cops?"

"Merciful heavens, *no!*" he gasped, staggering to a chair. He was suddenly only a tired, frightened old man. "I heard him refuse to give the letters to you," he said. "You were right. I shouldn't have tried to deal with them. But let them go. You understand I simply can't afford any publicity."

"This kills me!" I groaned. "It's the first time I ever let a crook go when I had him cold. But here goes. Outside, Wetzlaff!"

He went like a shorn lamb.

Gus and Joe threw the lot of them into their car. Bitters had made his escape. "Let's get going," I said. "A fadeout is the quickest way to hush it up."

Not until I was driving across the Lake Worth bridge did Trixie sigh contentedly.

"Mike, are we lucky, or aren't we? Everything fixed up— and both of us here safe and sound?"

"Not bad," says I.

"You said some sweet things on that island, Mike. I've been thinking about them ever since."

"Did I?" says I. "I had to think fast to break this case, didn't I? But I told you if you followed my orders we'd get somewhere."

Trixie moved away from me and blazed, "The next time I stroke a nitwit's ego I hope I'm caught dead! Listen to me, Mike Harris! Of all the conceited—"

Well, I had to drive and listen. It was the same old story. Trixie on my neck with her razor tongue for no reason at all. What a life! What a woman! I ask you.